JON TEEL
AND THE
MIRACLE
BUS

LANA LAWS DOWNING

ISBN 979-8-88616-561-6 (paperback)
ISBN 979-8-88616-562-3 (digital)

Christian Faith Publishing
832 Park Avenue
Meadville, PA 16335
www.christianfaithpublishing.com

Printed in the United States of America

BAKERVILLE

Fingers reaching from a dream tugged at the frayed blanket of sleep that protected Julia Hancock's tortured mind. She opened one eye tentatively, slowly remembering that she was in Bakerville General Hospital. Julia reached for her phone to check the date and time. Realization dawned. Today marked the one-year anniversary of the day Jon Teel had first arrived in Louisiana on a Greyhound bus. In the span of that year, life had changed for both Julia and Jon Teel in ways neither could have imagined.

Before the coming of Jon Teel, Julia knew before arising from her bed precisely what each new day would bring. She was a wealthy widow enjoying a somewhat boring life of privilege in a small southern town. The arrival of Jon Teel had changed her humdrum life into one of meaning. The boy's arrival had also brought Julia a great deal of danger and excitement.

Jon Teel had, in his few short years, lived through unspeakable torture and abuse, spending each day in fear. Then he met Julia who became his mentor, teacher, and savior while he became her reason for living. They had come through an unimaginable ordeal, sharing a bond that could not, would not, be broken.

An aide bustled into Julia's hospital room bearing a breakfast tray. A nurse entered the room to take vital signs, and then the laboratory technician brought a rolling cart laden with hypodermics and vials, ready to draw yet another sample of her blood. The nurse had the best news.

"Mrs. Julia, you're still pretty banged up, but your doctor says to get you ready to go home."

Home! The word had never sounded so good.

The men who had tortured Jon Teel had been captured but not before one of them, "Beast," aka Samuel Burleson, had thrown Julia against the brick wall of her home, leaving her with a concussion and broken ribs. Jon Teel had caused Beast's downfall—literally and figuratively—tripping him so that he fell headlong down the steep back stairs from the second floor of Julia's home. Law enforcement officers were waiting at the bottom to handcuff and shackle him and lead him away.

The other abuser was Jon Teel's own father, who went by the name of Jonathan Steelman, although law enforcement officials believed that was an alias. Both drug-dealing criminals were in the local jail awaiting trial, and then possible extradition to Texas, where they were wanted for several murders. Mexican authorities had also expressed an interest in the pair.

All Julia hoped and prayed for was that the two evildoers would be taken away from Bakerville for trial. Jon Teel had been through enough. He didn't need to see or hear about these malignant creatures ever again.

While she was in the hospital recovering from her injuries, Julia had asked for her iPad and started a list of things to do to ensure Jon Teel's well-being. First on that list was finding the best child psychologist she could locate in the area. She called upon the expertise of Dr. Elias Christian when he stopped by her hospital room.

"Julia, that's the first thing you really must do," he replied to her question. "In my opinion, the very best you can get is right over in New Iberia—the two Doctors Smith, Mary and William. They work together when necessary on difficult cases. I know your boy seems to have come through all this trauma unharmed, but I find that impossible to believe. I think he's stuffing his feelings way down deep, and they're bound to bubble up to the surface sometime. I'd like to see you head that off if you can. A good, gentle, probing psychologist who thoroughly understands all that Jon Teel has been through is going to be your best bet."

Julia typed on her iPad: "Things to Do." Number 1 was "Call the Doctors Smith."

She tried to list the items in descending order of importance. After the psychologists, she listed the following:

1. Call Judge Green and get an adoption lawyer who can assure that the adoption is ironclad.

2. Help Jon Teel select a permanent name for his official adoption and arrange for his baptism. See if the sheriff can learn Jon Teel's birthday from his father or from Beast.

3. Arrange to have the remains of Jon Teel's mother transferred from the forensic anthropologist in Baton Rouge to Bakerville for burial. Prepare a grave for the burial in the Hancock family plot.

4. Talk to Sheriff Blanchard about connections in Mexico to locate any relatives of Jon Teel and to head off any retaliation over the capture of Jon Teel's father, Jonathan Steelman, and his right-hand man, Beast.

5. Talk to the principal at St. John about enrolling Jon Teel for half days for his first few weeks of school.

Julia was anxious to get home from the hospital, but the doctors had insisted on keeping her for three nights because of the broken ribs and bruising to her lungs. The doctors were erring on the side of caution, keeping Julia hospitalized in order to avoid pneumonia. Her face was badly discolored, but Jon Teel paid no attention to it. He had seen his mother that way many times, Julia felt certain. His sweet young mother had probably pretended everything was fine as Julia was trying to do. Ultimately, Jon Teel's mother had paid with her life to save her son. Julia believed that Jon Teel's mother had suffered genuine martyrdom.

Jon Teel spent the three days with Julia at the hospital, going home with Florida and her girls at night.

"Julia, that boy doesn't cease to surprise me," Florida reported to Julia.

"He's like a different child. He talks to my girls so much that they can't get a word in edgewise. It's as though a faucet turned on when those animals got caught. We may be wishing we knew how to turn the faucet off! And such a vivid imagination! He insists that he saw Michael, the archangel, and that he prayed to his dead mama and that St. Michael and his mama worked together and helped him to trip up that Beast. He said that stair step made into a door was stuck tight, and St. Michael and his mama opened it for him. He also told the girls that he isn't sad about his mama because he sees her and talks to her all the time and

that she looks like an angel. She told him that she is his mother in heaven, but you would be his mother on earth, and we are all his family. What do you make of that?"

Julia didn't know what to make of it and said so.

"Flo, I guess it's his coping mechanism. Anything that helps him survive the things he has been through is fine by me."

Florida, Julia's friend and confidante since childhood, had been against inviting the boy into Julia's home as a foster child. Now, Florida had turned into Jon Teel's biggest fan and supporter. *Only a very hard heart could resist the innate sweetness in the child*, Julia thought as she considered more items that she should add to her list of things to do.

When she was finally released, Julia got into the wheelchair an aide brought to her room. Jon Teel walked along beside her to the hospital entrance as the nurse pushed the chair, keeping up a constant chatter about things Julia should and should not do. When they got to the entrance, Julia was amazed to see a crowd of well-wishers with flowers, balloons, and signs. A reporter from the television station that had broadcast Jon Teel's picture a year ago was there giving a play-by-play of Julia's release.

"Here she is, ladies and gentlemen, the woman of the hour, Bakerville's hometown heroine: Julia Chandler Hancock! She single-handedly faced down certain death to save the young abandoned child she had cared for and grown to love. Do you have any words, Mrs. Hancock?"

At that moment, out of the hospital parking lot, a huge man came running. Julia breathed a sigh of relief. It was J-Max. He jumped in front of the wheelchair and fielded the reporter's questions.

"Let's give Mrs. Julia some breathing space, guys. She's been through a terrible time. She has broken ribs and a concussion. It's hard for her to breathe much less go through an interview. I'm sure I can answer all your questions, and I'd be honored to do it."

J-Max, a well-known and popular figure, turned on his television commentator smile and charisma and soon had the television crew eating out of his hand. Julia, meanwhile, got into a vehicle provided by the sheriff's department. She and Jon Teel were on their way before the reporters knew they had departed.

Once again, J-Max had come to Julia's rescue. They had shared a strong bond since the time long ago when J-Max was Jamal—a struggling high school boy that Julia had tutored after diagnosing his severe dyslexia. He became an *A*-student, a local football hero, a star with the LSU Tigers, and then a highly successful pro football player. Now, he was a television football commentator during the season, spending the rest of his time in Bakerville with the

beloved, aged grandmother who had raised him. He was the most recognizable citizen in Bakerville.

The morning after Julia's homecoming, Jon Teel opened his eyes to golden morning light spilling into Julia's bedroom, giving the room a heavenly aura. Jon Teel had his own room, but his little bed was next to Julia's for sleeping to give the child security while they were under threat.

He blinked rapidly, assuring himself that he was awake, and this was real. He rolled over to peer through the slats of his little bed, checking to be sure Julia was really there. She was there, looking right back at him. He drew in a breath, exhaled, and reached over to touch Julia's arm. The two of them burst into peals of joyous laughter—a pair of happy humans who had escaped the clutches of evil. Jon Teel believed he was safe and that he might, finally, lose the knot that had gripped his body ever since he had memory.

Julia reached over to grasp his small hand, wiping away tears of laughter and joy. Her heart filled until she felt actual pain in her chest. She had been exceedingly joyful on her wedding day, but this was different. She and this beautiful boy had come through hell relatively unscathed. Now that she was home, Julia felt that she could finally breathe—albeit with the pain of the broken ribs. Awaking in her own bed to laugh with Jon Teel was the best medicine she could want.

After she and Jon Teel finished with their happy giggling, they noticed the clatter of dishes and pans coming from the kitchen. While Julia limped into the bathroom to shower, Jon Teel raced downstairs in his pajamas to greet Florida.

"Miss Florida, we're home, and everything is okay!"

His small face shone with joy. Florida wondered to herself how she could ever have wanted to turn this child away. She prayed every night for forgiveness. She grabbed Jon Teel in a tight hug.

"Yes, Jon, everything is really going to be okay. Now, how about some breakfast? Anything you want.

"Pancakes and bacon!"

Before the capture of the villains, the child would not have asked for breakfast. His answer would have been a shrug of his shoulders, and Florida would have set a plate of food before him. Generally, he ate at least a few bites. Now, Florida was gratified to see that he did, indeed, have favorite dishes that he would be happy to make known, and he had an excellent appetite.

When Julia came down, over a light breakfast, she decided to tackle the issue of a new name head-on. She didn't mind Jon, but the Teel part might have to go. She was certain that Teel was a derivative of Steelman, his biological father's surname. Julia felt this name change could be important to the process of letting go of his horrendous past. Plus, she didn't want the name of Jonathan Steelman associated with her son.

"Jon," she began, "we need to finalize your adoption and see about getting you baptized. Your mother may have baptized you, but we can't be sure. Have you thought about a name that you like? You should choose a good middle name, and your last name will be Hancock, like my name. Do you understand?"

"I understand," he replied, sounding more mature than his age, "but first, there's something more important. What should I call you, Julia?"

Julia hadn't thought about it since he had called her "*Mami nueva*"—new mommy—at the hospital.

"Well, I'll give you some choices. You may call me Julia, or you may call me mama, mommy, mother, or Mama Julia. Do you like any of those?"

He thought hard for a time, his brow wrinkled with the effort.

"I like Mama Julia, or maybe Mama J."

"I like both of those, and I'll answer to any of them. As long as you promise to call me any time you need me. Now, there's the question of a name for you. Have you thought about it?"

"I did think about it when you were in the hospital when I stayed with Orlie and Waveland. They said your husband was named John but not spelled like my name Jon. But I think I have the same name as your husband anyway. *J-o-n* or *J-o-h-n*, it's the same. I don't want to change my name. It's what my mami called me, and it's what my family in Mexico will know if they look for me—my *abuelos* and my mami's *abuelita*. I saw her only once, but my mami loved her very much. She's tiny like a little child, but she has a great big heart. She talks to me sometimes, in my dreams, when I'm sleeping. I want my name to stay the same so my family can find me if they look."

Julia felt a sense of foreboding. The thought that Jon Teel's relatives might come looking for him hadn't occurred to her. Another worry to add to her list. Suddenly, Julia felt overcome. She felt John's presence in the house at that moment, knowing Jon Teel had considered her late husband in choosing to keep his name.

"All right then, we'll call you Jon Teel. Now, what about a middle name?"

"I think I'll choose Michael because he defends us in battle. I like to see Michael the archangel stabbing the devil with his big sword.

I prayed that he would help me in the little room under the stairs when I heard Beast coming, and he and my mami came and helped me because that was a battle. His sword helped me to get that step open and make it stay. Orlie and Waveland say it was a miracle that I could make Beast trip, and I know it's because Michael, the archangel, was there."

These long bursts of conversation continued to amaze Julia considering that the child had been mostly silent for nearly a year. In addition, she was surprised at his matter-of-fact assumption of divine intervention. This was a demonstration of strong faith at a very young age.

"Yes, I do believe your quick thinking was a minor miracle. In fact, I think you are my miracle boy. I will thank your sweet mother in heaven every day. I think she must be one of God's favorites. And, Jon, I am so proud of your name choices and your reasons for them! You will be Jon Teel Michael Hancock beginning today. And I'll call the rectory to arrange for your baptism. Who do you want for godparents?"

Again, the child amazed Julia. It seemed that this too had been discussed with Florida's girls.

"I want three godmothers: Miss Florida, Orlie, and Waveland. I want one godfather: J-Max."

"I couldn't have chosen better myself," Julia exclaimed, hugging the child close.

After a phone call to the rectory, the baptism was set for the following Sunday after ten thirty Mass. Florida joined in the discussion.

"We surely need to have a little party after," Florida said. "We'll get you a real bakery cake—whatever kind you want—and we can have sandwiches and punch. Who else do you want to invite?"

"I want DJ, of course."

DJ was Daniel Henry Jones—ostensibly Julia's gardener, but, in reality—her right-hand person for security around Dapplefield Manor. He was their bodyguard and trusted friend.

"And I want J-Max's grandmother if she can come and the sheriff and Dr. Christian and Judge Green. I wish my *abuelos* could come, my grandparents in Mexico and *Abuelita, abuela's* mother."

The more Julia heard, the more she realized that this had been discussed at length in the evenings Jon Teel had spent at Florida's home with the girls while Julia was recuperating in the hospital. The child's strong sense of the spiritual was part of his nature. It was evident that this spiritual sense had come from his martyred mother, the young Maria Maristella. Julia had decided to follow her instincts and speak often to the boy about his mother, always praising her and reaffirming the way that she had protected her child. She wanted to keep his young mother's memory alive in her son.

They went to sit in the sunroom, and together, in that beautiful setting facing the rolling lawn that ended at the bayou side, they planned the baptismal party.

"Mama J, I want to have part of the party outside so we can have some games. I never had a real party, and really, my baptism day is like a birthday, isn't it?"

Again, the child's wisdom surprised Julia. She and Florida exchanged glances. Florida spoke up.

"That's a fine idea. We'll have a baptism birthday cake with candles. Your baptism day will be your birthday until we find out when your real birthday is. Yes, we can have some games and presents, and we'll sing happy birthday, and you'll blow out your candles."

"How many candles will you put, Miss Florida?"

"Why don't you call me Aunt Flo? And Waveland and Orlie can be your big sisters or cousins or whatever you need them to be. We'll all be a crazy mixed-up family. We'll put lots of candles. We won't worry about how many. Let's plan your games. How about Pin the Tail on the Donkey? And how about a piñata?"

The child's eyes widened when the word *piñata* was mentioned.

"How do you know about piñatas, Miss Flo, I mean, Aunt Flo? I saw one when I went to Mexico with Mami to get a package. I would like a piñata, but I want to pick it out. I don't want to beat up Batman or Spiderman. When my cousins in Mexico beat up the Spiderman piñata and it broke open, I started to cry. I want one that isn't a live thing. Maybe a watermelon or a banana or a cactus."

They all laughed at that, but Julia latched onto his comment about having been in Mexico with his mother.

"Jon, did you go to Mexico every time your mami went?"

"Of course. Mami would never leave me alone with those people."

"Those people" included his own father. Julia was glad to realize that the boy did not think of Jonathan Steelman as his father.

"Did your mami visit her family when she was there?"

"Oh yes. I saw my *abuelos* and even *Abuela's* own mother. I told you that she is very old! She really is very small too, only a little taller than I am. We call her *Abuelita*—little grandmother."

Julia needed time to process the fact that the child really did have a family in Mexico including grandparents and a great-grandmother.

"And I have *tias* and *tios* and some *primos*."

He also had aunts and uncles and some cousins. The plot was thickening. Julia knew she needed to speak to Sheriff Blanchard and Judge Porteous Green as soon as possible to try to get some information out of Mexico. There was a large family that might want Maria Maristella's child

returned to them. So much to do! And so many unanswered questions. There was no official record of the child's birth, but there was reason to believe he had been born on American soil in the drug cartel's boatshed hideout near Houston.

SALTILLO

A twelve-hour drive south from Bakerville but a world away, a short indigenous man named Juan Diego Garcia-Hernandez made his weekly rounds in Saltillo, Mexico. He took his gentle old donkey, Bonita, hitched her to his ancient cart, and left his lean-to home. His home and his small workshop were nestled in a rocky gorge off the major highway that went south from Laredo to Saltillo. Juan Diego never rode on Bonita. He loved and respected the old donkey too much. Instead, he walked beside her, keeping up a steady stream of conversation.

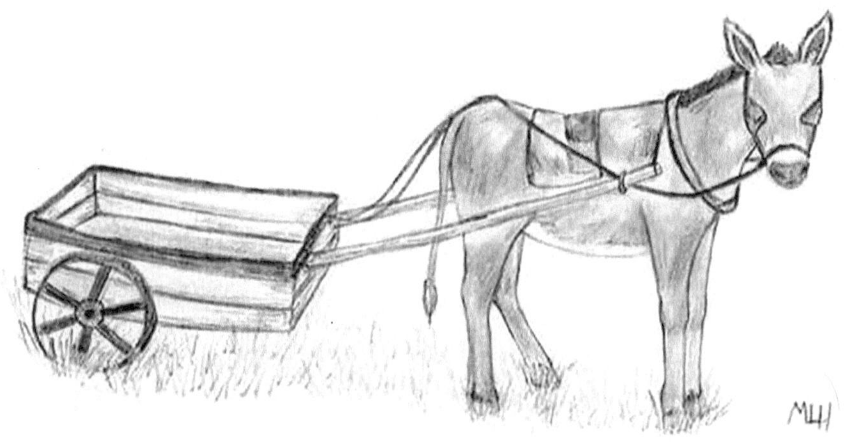

He often considered his soul, the unseen part of himself, what he thought of as his spiritual self. He believed this part of himself to be organized on two levels like a two-story house. On the first floor of the house that was his mind-soul, he dealt with the world on a minute-by-minute basis, meeting and solving problems along the way. This was where he decided whether to stop at this place or that one, whether to eat beans or not.

There was a second much grander floor in his house. It was on this level, he believed, that he recognized the beauty in God's world, wondered at the colors on the butterfly that landed on Bonita's straw hat, or the ability of the hummingbird to fly backward and forward among the flowers. This was where he met with God, telling him his problems, and asking for his help. He tried to remember to give thanks every day. He loved to spend time on the second floor of the house that was his spiritual self as he walked alongside Bonita.

Today, he looked down at his dusty calloused feet and said, "I thank you, Father, for giving me the skill to make these shoes to cover my feet so I can walk to town."

He spent a good deal of time on the second floor of his spiritual house as he walked along, ruminating on God's plan for a lowly man such as himself in the big, beautiful world filled with people more important, intelligent, and powerful than he. Then he returned to the first floor of his house where practical thoughts prevailed.

"What do you think we will find today, Bonita? We need some more sheet metal for the roof, but that's hard to come by. Maybe a can with paint left in it? Every day is a treasure hunt because it's always a surprise. God is good to us, Bonita."

Juan Diego was a humble man. His needs were few, mostly provided by the farms around his home or by his foraging expeditions. He wore old khaki pants held up by a rope belt. His shirt was coarse blue cotton. His shoes were his own creation. He had found an old pair of sturdy work boots at the Saltillo dump. He had cut away all the top leather except for the thick black rubber sole and the back portion that covered his heel. He put a tough thong of leather through the sole between his toes, connected to a leather band with lacing around his ankle. He didn't know it, but his design was very close to the shoes worn by his ancestors six hundred years previously before the coming of the Spaniards.

On they walked, stopping first at the magnificent cathedral, Catedral de Santiago, the St. James Cathedral. This was Juan Diego's favorite place in all of Saltillo. Designed in a mixture of exuberant architectural styles, built over decades beginning in the sixteenth century after the Spaniards came, the cathedral had splendid stone carvings, magnificent art masterpieces, impressive altars. Juan Diego was especially fond of the image of Santo Cristo de la Cana made with the cane of corn plants. Juan Diego was at heart an artist and artisan; he appreciated the work of talented creators, especially those who worked with whatever materials they could find.

Today, he didn't enter the cathedral, not wanting to leave his beloved Bonita unattended. On Sunday, he would return for the early Mass to hear the bishop's homily. He was a great fan of the man, Bishop Jose´ Gilberto Lopez, who defended poor people and fought for their rights without ceasing. This gained the bishop no popularity among the wealthy and powerful citizens of Saltillo nor among members of the burgeoning drug cartels.

Juan Diego led Bonita around to the back of the huge cathedral structure into a back alley where trash was placed for collection. This was one of his favorite hunting sites, sometimes yielding amazing treasures. Today, he found a small cache of religious items. This was a rare find as such artifacts were not generally thrown away. The careless act of a custodian of the cathedral was a windfall for Juan Diego. In a plastic shopping bag, he found a small broken statue of the Virgin of Guadalupe and a dozen or so metal *milagros*—miniature metal charms representing hands, feet, eyes, automobiles, and animals, anything for which a person might pray for healing or help. The milagros could be bought for pennies to attach to the cloth garments of statues in the cathedral. In Mexico City, the faithful still walked on their knees across the huge square to the church built in honor of the Virgin of Guadalupe, often carrying the milagros with which they would petition

the Virgin for help with their various problems with their health, finances, marriage, and children.

Juan Diego had a great devotion to the Virgin of Guadalupe. It was his lifelong dream to make a pilgrimage to her shrine. According to his grandfather, now long dead, Juan Diego was a direct descendant of the first Juan Diego to whom the Virgin had appeared in 1531. When Juan Diego was a boy, his grandfather had recited his lineage through the centuries. As he remembered it today, that family tree sounded suspiciously like the lineage of Jesus from the Bible readings at Christmastime. True or not, Juan Diego took great pride in his connection to the Virgin of Guadalupe.

He reached into the bag he had found and pulled out the small statue. It was mostly intact, with only a few chips in the plaster, but her beautiful face had been damaged. Juan Diego kissed her feet and spoke aloud:

"Dear little Virgin Maria, do not worry! I can fix you up better than ever!"

He put her back into the plastic sack which he placed carefully in his tattered cloth bag.

Juan Diego had no idea that he had a silent observer. Bishop Jose´ Gilberto Lopez—always vigilant, constantly observing the goings-on in his diocese—stood at an upstairs window in his study where it was his habit to read

his breviary and recite the rosary every day. Now, however, he stood mesmerized watching the short unassuming little man unhurriedly sorting through the rubbish outside the back entrance of the cathedral. He sighed when he saw what had been thoughtlessly discarded. Thanks to his new prescription eyeglasses, he could see quite clearly. There was a system in place in the cathedral to dispose of unwanted religious items with respect. They were not to be thrown into the garbage, not to be unceremoniously loaded onto a filthy garbage truck and hauled to the city dump.

Today, however, he felt an unseen hand at work when he observed the little man, obviously descended from the indigenous people native to the area, as he reverently held the small Guadalupe statue, kissed her feet while he spoke to her, and gently placed her safely into his bag for transport. The bishop made a mental note to tell the staff to save such items and put them in a place where the foraging man could find them. Here was an opportunity for recycling at its best.

Juan Diego grasped Bonita's harness, and the two of them ambled away, headed for their next stop which was the city's dumping grounds. This was all in a day's work for the pair.

Juan Diego had taken many duties upon his shoulders. It seemed he was busy night and day. Near his makeshift home was an encampment of recent arrivals: poor people who wanted their presence kept in strict secrecy. Juan Diego had been taking helpful items to the little group including scraps of food, bits of cloth, anything that might help them survive. Over the span of many weeks, he gained their trust and learned that they were the remaining relatives, distant cousins, aunts, and uncles, of Maria Maristella Lopez, mother of Jon Teel.

Everyone in northern Mexico had heard the story of young Maria Maristella—the beautiful fourteen-year-old girl sold by her father to a drug lord. The hapless father sacrificed his beautiful young daughter to save his remaining family.

In the end, it didn't matter. When Maria Maristella betrayed him, taking her young son from the cartel's hideout near Houston to Louisiana on a Greyhound bus, the drug kingpin, Jonathan Steelman, had her tortured and murdered by his right-hand man, Beast. Steelman continued to pull strings from his prison cell in the United States. His underlings hunted her parents and siblings down and executed them in the cruelest fashion the cartels had yet devised.

First, he had his henchmen take the children, younger brothers and sisters of Maria Maristella, bind their hands and feet and stand them inside a stack of tires reaching to their shoulders. They doused them with gasoline and set them on fire as their parents—themselves bound, gagged and immobile—watched in unspeakable horror, hearing the screams of their children, smelling the burning flesh and the stench of the rubber tires, as they awaited the same gruesome fate.

Onlookers claimed that they never had another good night of sleep after witnessing the terrible fate of the family and seeing firsthand the cruelty that one human being was capable of inflicting on another. The drug lords got their message across.

The worst of it was that the murderers committed their crimes in the name of their twisted religion—a devotion to Santa Muerte, the embodiment of death. They venerated the skeletal image of the goddess, made offerings to her, and used her as the excuse for their terrible acts. Satan was alive and acting through these individuals.

Juan Diego knew that Maria Maristella's grandmother was hiding out with the ragtag group camped near his home. One day, as he delivered a few bits of food he had collected from a kind restaurant owner, together with a tattered old shawl made at the factory in Saltillo, he gathered his courage and asked one of the older men if he might meet the grandmother of Maria Maristella. He chose his words carefully.

"My friend, I know that you are taking care of the grandmother of the little saint Maria Maristella. I have such admiration for the girl. She gave her life to save her son. Not many have the courage to do such a thing. I will never reveal her grandmother's whereabouts, not even if they threaten to kill me."

The man looked Juan Diego up and down, assessing his sincerity and his trustworthiness. Juan Diego had certainly tried to help them, giving them food, building materials, clothing that he picked up scavenging the streets of Saltillo. Certainly, if he had wanted to turn them in to the cartels or reveal their whereabouts, he would have done so by this time. He indicated that Juan Diego should follow him into a large, tattered tent.

As Juan Diego's eyes adjusted to the dim light inside, he saw a small figure sitting in a corner, a large shawl wrapped around her thin shoulders. Juan Diego approached the seated woman. The tiny grandmother looked up to greet him, her wrinkled lips forming a gentle smile. But her eyes caught Juan Diego off guard. They were dark, liquid pools of such depth that Juan Diego had the sensation that she could see into his soul and read his innermost thoughts. Her eyes revealed profound sadness. The little grandmother must know the terrible fate that had befallen her murdered family.

In those moments of introduction, Juan Diego decided that the deaths of her poor family members must count for something. This poor woman should not be left to languish in a tent on the side of a highway. Maria Maristella should be a saint with her statue in the cathedral, and her grandmother should be reunited with Maria Maristella's son, Jon Teel, in Louisiana. All these thoughts jumbled together in Juan Diego's mind. He didn't know how to make it all happen, but he knew he must try.

*****

The bishop of Saltillo was well-aware of the presence of the cult of Santa Muerte in the region. He also knew almost immediately of the murders of the family members of the poor martyred girl Maria Maristella Lopez. He promised himself that he would learn what he could about the whole tragic affair because of his firm belief that the girl could be a candidate for sainthood. He was ruminating over all of this as he looked out of his study window. It was a Monday morning, the time when the odd little scavenging man generally appeared to rummage through the cathedral trash.

Sure enough, as though on cue, Bonita and Juan Diego rounded the corner into the alley behind the cathedral.

"Fernando!" The bishop called to the young priest who was his secretary and general right-hand man.

"Go down to the alleyway and tell that gentleman that I wish to see him immediately. Have him come into the courtyard with his donkey and cart. He won't leave them unattended, and I don't blame him."

Father Fernando looked out the window to see what had the bishop's attention. An expression of distaste crossed his usually impassive face.

"Your excellency, are you sure…"

"Yes, yes, Fernando, I am sure. And bring up the bag of items I had the housekeeper put into the pantry for the gentleman who scavenges."

Without further comment, Father Fernando left to do the bishop's bidding.

Juan Diego was immediately afraid when the tall gentleman approached, obviously a priest of some importance, dressed in a long black cassock. He figured he must be in trouble, possibly accused of theft. He began preparing his defense. Trash was trash, in the public domain, free for the taking. He hoped it would work on church property.

"You must follow me," the tall priest said, leaving no room for dissent. He turned to lead the way into the fenced and gated courtyard.

"Bring your animal and your cart. They will be safe here."

Juan Diego didn't appreciate his calling Bonita an animal, but he grabbed her harness and picked up her reins, and they followed the man through the gate.

"There is water and a place to tie the animal up," the man said, pointing to a half barrel of rainwater.

Juan Diego silently obeyed. Bonita took a long drink of water and began to nibble on the grass that grew between the flagstones of the courtyard. Juan Diego appreciated the priest's concern for Bonita.

"Come with me," the tall priest said.

They entered the back door of the bishop's residence and ascended the back stairway to an upstairs hall. The bishop's study was just off the hall. He stood waiting for them to arrive.

"You may leave us, Father Fernando," the bishop said, "and please shut the door on your way out."

The bishop felt a bit guilty about what he had in mind, and he didn't want anyone to know what he was going to do. He had decided to enlist the aid of the most common citizen he could find to help him glean information. A man such as this one, out every day going through the city looking for usable trash, was just the ticket. He was inconspicuous, practically invisible. He would naturally hear things.

He could be an immense help in learning what the bishop wanted to know. The bishop looked Juan Diego up and down, taking note of his tattered though relatively clean clothes, his crude homemade sandals, and his calloused hands and feet.

"My good man," the bishop began, "I have seen you on several occasions going through the trash generated from the cathedral—"

"Oh, your excellency, I am so sorry—" Juan Diego stammered the beginning of an explanation.

"No, no, you misunderstand," the bishop said, "I am happy for you to make use of what is discarded. In fact, I have put aside a large bag of such items for you. No, I intend to ask a favor of you in the hope that you might be able to help me. Have you heard of the vicious murders of the family of young Maria Maristella? The girl killed by the drug cartel that traffics in this area?"

Juan Diego was thunderstruck. How much did this powerful man know? Could he possibly know about the little grandmother hiding out near Juan Diego's own home? He thought for a few moments before answering.

"Your Excellency, all of Saltillo and all of this region has heard of the murders, first of the poor girl and then her family. Those evil people want the world to know of their terrible crimes. They do these things in the name of Santa

Muerte, all to make the people afraid to go against them. They are very, very bad people."

Juan Diego paused and crossed himself before continuing.

"This is the most terrible evil. All the people are afraid of these crazy bad men and Santa Muerte. They take the young men into their culture of crime and death. Even the police are afraid of them."

"Yes, yes, I know this," the bishop replied, a bit impatiently, "but I want to know what you hear of the affair. And what do the people think? Are there any family members of the poor murdered girl left alive? If there are, I believe it is the duty of Holy Mother Church to give them our protection."

Juan Diego considered what he should say. He was afraid to reveal too much. He knew this man by reputation, and he appreciated his thoughtful homilies at Mass, but that didn't mean he could be trusted. He might accidentally reveal information that would lead the bad people directly to the hiding place of Maria Maristella's grandmother.

"Your excellency, the evil men have vowed to avenge their two leaders who are in American prisons. They will kill anyone connected to Maria Maristella. They killed the poor girl in a very cruel manner from what I heard. She suffered greatly before she died. All she wanted to do was save her young son from a life in the drug cartels. They killed Maria Maristella, and then they found her mother and father and all her brothers and sisters and executed them with the necktie of fire. They bound them and burned them alive. Their screams still echo at the murdering place, the local people say. I think it would mean death to anyone left alive in that family if their whereabouts were revealed. The walls of the church would not protect that person. At least that is what I believe."

The bishop had a sense that this was an unusually long speech for Juan Diego. The little man seemed to be interested in the case of Maria Maristella and her unfortunate family. Juan Diego might be just the person the bishop was looking for to help him learn what the authorities could not. The bishop couldn't trust the police to get the information he sought. There was always a mole in the police station who would send word back to the drug cartels, always someone willing to betray innocent people for money.

"All I want to know," the bishop said amicably, "is whether or not any member of the family is still alive and how we might help them, perhaps to escape to the United States. I understand that Maria Maristella's young son is living there in safety. I would like to do the same for anyone else in the family, to get them to safety and possibly reunite them with the boy in Louisiana. All I am asking is that you keep your ear to the ground as you make your rounds. No one is in a better position than a person such as yourself who sees many people in a day. The authorities can't do it because their every move is reported to the cartels, but you might hear something. If you do, I'd like to know. No one will be the wiser because it will appear that I am only helping you by giving you the cathedral's discards. You can let me know if you hear anything. I am in contact with the bishop of the diocese of Lafayette in Louisiana where the young boy lives. That bishop too is interested in the case. We both believe young Maria to be a worthy case for sainthood. If there is anything we can do to further the cause and protect her family, we are willing to do it. Will you agree to help me?"

"Bishop, it's possible I can find out information for you. I can only promise that I will try. I'll be back every Monday. If I learn anything, I'll look up to your window and give a sign."

Juan Diego departed and traveled as usual toward the main rubbish disposal grounds of Saltillo. His heart was pounding. The bishop couldn't possibly know about the little grandmother, could he? Juan Diego wasn't ready to reveal her location to anyone, not even the bishop. What if the bishop inadvertently let it slip and the bad people found her? They would all face certain death. He needed a

real plan before he let the bishop in on his massive secret. He hoped it didn't count as a lie to the bishop to say that he would try when he already knew the answer.

He and Bonita arrived at the dump, a huge pile of garbage and waste, mostly trash of no value but a source of hidden treasures if a person were observant and diligent enough to find them. He ruminated over the astounding meeting with the bishop as he searched the piles of rubble. Today, Juan Diego found a few discarded cans of aluminum paint with usable amounts left in the bottom of each of them.

"Probably from the government," he mused. He believed "the government" to be very wasteful. Looking further, he found partial loaves of stale bread, a cache of hard avocados that might possibly ripen, and several short lengths of rusty corrugated sheet metal. He could use all of it, or he could share it with his secretive neighbors who had in their midst the very person the bishop sought: the grandmother of the murdered Maria Maristella.

He loaded the items he found into Bonita's cart next to the large bag the bishop had given him. It contained fresh *bolillos*, crusty rolls that were very tasty, several yards of coarse blue fabric, some small paint brushes, a nearly new warm blanket, and a small paperbound Holy Bible. He felt like the luckiest person in all of Saltillo.

The humblest of men, Juan Diego had neither the education nor the vocabulary to put his various thoughts and visions into words. His agile mind was filled with many ideas, dreams, and ambitions, most of them nebulous, but all aimed at helping others. He would need assistance with his latest plan to save the little grandmother, so he had been praying daily to St. Anthony to find someone to come to his aid. He was developing a vague plan involving a windfall that had come his way some months previously. He wondered if the bishop might be the person God had sent to help him make use of the gift that had come his way.

*****

Some months earlier, Juan Diego was gathering firewood on the side of the big highway when an ancient school bus came lumbering along. In crude hand-painted lettering, the words "Temple of the Spirit Tabernacle Church" were emblazoned across the side with the name of the bus's former school district visible underneath the thin coat of paint.

Gears grinding, the bus slowed and pulled off the main road following the sandy path Juan Diego and Bonita had carved out through hundreds of foraging trips into the city of Saltillo. Juan Diego watched from a hidden spot in the cedar shrubbery to see what the interlopers were up to. The driver turned off the engine. The bus gave a shudder, a belch of exhaust, and fell silent. Then the driver slumped over the steering wheel, appearing to be unconscious or dead. Juan Diego was horrified. The lone passenger, an elderly man, moved from his seat to stand beside the driver. He began to scream.

"Help! Somebody, help!"

Juan Diego sprang from his hiding place and ran to the bus door.

The passenger reached into the driver's shirt pocket and pulled out a flip phone. He opened the bus door and reached out to hand the phone to Juan Diego.

"Please, sir, take this phone and call for help!"

"No, no, I am not able," Juan Diego replied, "I know nothing of telephones. You must call. I will tend to the driver."

The passenger appeared relieved to leave the unconscious man and the bus. He pulled the key from the bus's ignition and handed the keychain off to Juan Diego.

"Keep these safe," he said, "I don't want the bus to be stolen."

Odd, Juan Diego mused, *how does he know I, myself, won't steal it?*

The passenger walked up to the highway, phone in hand, speaking rapidly. Juan Diego couldn't hear everything, but he did hear the words *emergency, maybe dead,* and the approximate location.

When the man returned to the bus, he and Juan Diego checked on the driver and decided that he was, in fact, dead. The thin, gray-haired passenger had recovered from his earlier distress and did not seem to be overly concerned.

"We pass from this life to a better place," he said with a stoic shrug.

Then the passenger and Juan Diego had a rapid-fire conversation. Apparently, the passenger from the bus revealed, there was a problem with the license or registration of the bus. Because of this, the passenger, who identified himself simply as Raphael, came up with a plan of action.

"Sir, you appear to be a trustworthy man. I must entrust to you the care of this bus. My pastor bought it and paid for it on good faith, but there was a problem with the registration. So far, the bus is still in the name of the last owner who turned out to be a scoundrel of the worst sort. I believe it is in our best interest to remove the pastor's body from the bus and take him to the side of the road. I will tell the authorities we were hitch hiking, and the pastor was suddenly stricken. I will tell them that the truck driver who gave us a ride left us on the side of the road not wanting to be involved in the matter of a death in his vehicle because he was on a tight schedule. I cannot remember anything about the truck because I was in such terrible distress. You, sir, will be left out of the situation entirely. This bus was bought at great cost by this good dead man to be used for God's purposes, not to go to the police junkyard or back into the hands of the previous owner who has already been paid. This bus has more work to do for the Lord. I leave it in your hands."

Juan Diego could see the logic of the proposal. Anything that kept the authorities out of one's business was invariably the best course of action. As this was outside the limits of the city of Saltillo, it would be the *federales*, the government police, who would respond. The two men acted quickly. First, Raphael located a worn blanket on the bus and placed it on the ground a few yards from the highway. Then, working together, they painstakingly carried the body of the driver and placed it on the blanket. Thankfully, the dead man's eyes were closed. They respectfully folded his hands over his chest, mumbled a quick Our Father, and backed away from the body.

"Now, my new friend, you must hide yourself. There is no need for you to be involved. Just take care of the bus."

With that, Raphael walked back to stand beside the dead body. He turned to wave at Juan Diego. He made a shooing motion indicating that Juan Diego should move himself and the bus out of sight. They could hear the strident sound of sirens in the distance approaching rapidly.

Juan Diego got behind the wheel of the bus, hesitantly turned the key to start the engine, put it into gear, and moved it further down the path where it was hidden from view. He had little experience with driving and certainly no experience driving such a large vehicle, but he managed to do it. Then he found a vantage point from which to observe.

The *federales* arrived in full force. There was an armed Jeep, a patrol car, and an ambulance. They checked the body to ascertain that the man was truly dead. They examined the body for signs of foul play and, finding nothing to indicate otherwise, decided that it was a natural death. The man's wallet contained his driver's license, which provided his name. They ran it through the electronic system and learned that he was a church pastor with no outstanding charges, criminal or otherwise, against him. The ambulance attendants wrapped the body in a sheet and loaded it into the ambulance for the trip to the morgue.

After a brief conversation with the officer in charge, punctuated with much gesticulation, Raphael climbed into

the ambulance to ride along with the body. He stole a surreptitious glance in the direction of Juan Diego's hiding place giving a little wave and a big wink as he closed the back door of the vehicle. Then the entourage drove slowly and silently away.

That had been at least six months ago. Juan Diego began to think the events of that strange day were the result of divine intervention. Having heard nothing further from Raphael, he began to believe that he, Juan Diego, was the owner of a school bus. He had no doubt that the school bus was destined to do the Lord's work.

He wondered why he had heard nothing from Raphael, the mysterious passenger. He began to develop the idea that Raphael was not a man at all, but Raphael the archangel, who had come down from heaven in a human skin to give the bus to Juan Diego. Tentatively, he began to dream of what he might do with such an unbelievable gift from above. He decided that if the coming of the bus was an act of divine intervention, he was duty bound to use it for a good purpose.

An outlandish plan began to develop in his fertile imagination.

BAKERVILLE

In Bakerville, plans for the baptism/birthday celebration accelerated. Florida located a cactus piñata and Mexican-themed paper party goods to honor Jon Teel's mother's heritage. She decided that they must have a cake from Corrie the Cake Lady. Corrie had the imagination to take their idea and run with it. She was a magician with icing and cake decor. The cake was bound to be spectacular. Jon Teel decided he wanted a Michael the archangel cake, a first for Corrie, but she agreed to do it. All she needed was a small statue of St. Michael from The Rosary House in New Iberia, some plastic swords, and some gold circles for halos.

After a conversation with Florida, Corrie was on a mission. This would be her best baptism-birthday cake ever. They decided on three layers with chocolate filling and fluffy white icing to resemble clouds. The swords represented St. Michael's fighting spirit. The gold halos stood for his holiness. Corrie would use her biggest pans. Money was no object. Jon Teel danced around the kitchen in anticipation of the marvelous cake.

They ordered finger sandwiches from the Forest Restaurant. Al Kuhlman would handle the order personally. This was a first for Florida who held the firm belief that homemade was always best. However, the party required dozens of sandwiches, and she would be too busy to make them. Fruit punch with sherbet floating in it filled out the menu—all designed to meet the wishes of Jon Teel.

On Sunday morning, Florida and her girls arrived at Julia's home early enough for a get-together around the Wise Sayings box. The box had been in Julia's family for generations with an ever-growing store of proverbs and good advice stored within it on scraps of paper. There was no argument today about who would reach into the old cypress box and choose the saying of the day. Jon Teel reached in and picked a piece of tissue-thin blue paper with old-fashioned script written in blue ink. He handed it to Orlie to read.

> Trust in the Lord with all your heart,
> and do not rely on your own insight. In
> all your ways acknowledge him and he
> will make straight your paths. (Proverbs
> 3:5–6)

"Oh! Oh!" Jon Teel squealed, "The path will be straight for Abuelita to come!"

The little group remained quiet, digesting the odd remark from Jon Teel. His great-grandmother was still occupying his thoughts. Julia wondered why he never mentioned Maria Maristella's parents and siblings, but she didn't want to spoil the moment by asking. She put it out of her mind, and the group walked over to church for Mass and the baptism of Jon Teel. The beautiful church, a short walk down Main Street from Julia's home, never failed to inspire Julia and lift her thoughts heavenward.

Father had rearranged the music schedule so that the choir could sing for the Mass before the baptism of Jon Teel. Their repertoire and their voices were inspired. Father's homily was also inspired, touching on the serendipitous nature of life and how being open to change could enrich one's life in unexpected ways. He looked directly at Julia, smiling as he made this point.

When Mass ended, Father invited the congregation to stay to witness the baptismal ceremony. This surprised Julia. She had mixed feelings about having an audience, but it made Jon Teel so happy that she forgot her misgivings. She was in the habit of shielding the boy from attention of any kind. Nearly everyone in attendance at Mass stayed to watch Jon Teel's baptism which turned out to be a moving ceremony.

His chosen godfather J-Max was a hero in the town. He lifted the boy in his arms as easily as though he were a kitten. He held him for the pouring of the water on his head. Jon Teel was so solemn and attentive throughout the brief ceremony that the entire congregation felt that they were in the presence of special holiness. That day, the church parish adopted the boy as their own.

The party was a rousing success. Julia was glad that Corrie had insisted on an extra-large cake. Many in the congregation who had witnessed the baptism interpreted Father's invitation to remain for the ceremony to extend to the party afterward. Most of the congregation followed the entourage as they walked the short distance from the church to Julia's backyard for the celebration. Like the loaves and the fishes, there seemed to be enough food for everyone. Julia was happy to have the extra children to join in the games. In addition, Jon Teel might have a few friends when he began formal school classes.

The smallest girl in the group broke the *piñata* on her first mighty swing. The children scrambled after the sweets that fell to the ground. Jon Teel joined right in as though he had been a member of the group since birth.

The squeals of happy laughter were like silver bells tinkling at Christmastime to Julia's ears.

The sheriff and his wife, Judge Green and Dr. and Mrs. Christian, all attended the party. J-Max brought his grand-mother which delighted Jon Teel because she reminded him of his little great-grandmother in Mexico.

*****

Jon Teel began attending school in the morning, returning home at lunchtime. Either Florida or Julia walked the short distance to accompany him to school and to get him at noon. He entered at second grade level, but the principal called Julia on Thursday of the first week to report that the boy should be moved up.

"Mrs. Hancock, your homeschooling must have been top-notch. I am recommending that we move Jon to third grade," the principal said.

Julia readily agreed. Dr. Christian believed Jon Teel to be about eight years old despite his small size. She certainly didn't want the boy bored in school. He was doing well at St. John. There had been an incident with a bully, but Jon Teel had been dealing since his birth with much bigger bullies. He knew that the best defense was no offense. He simply did not engage with the offending child. The other students came to his aid, and the bully backed off. The name-calling ended as quickly as it began.

Jon Teel recounted the incident when Julia asked him about it, having heard from the principal that there had been a bit of trouble.

"Mama J, don't worry. It was nothing. That boy tries it on everyone. I'm easy because I'm not big. But I don't let bullies make me afraid. That's what they want. To make people scared of them. If you don't let them, they don't know what to do. I think that boy has a bad life."

The boy's sensitive, intuitive nature never failed to impress Julia. Jon Teel's days at St. John were mostly peaceful and happy. By the second week, he was a third grader attending school all day. Julia began to consider inviting a few classmates over after school.

The little hidden room under the stairs became Jon Teel's private sanctuary. When he returned from school each day, he had a snack in the kitchen while he recounted the events of the day for Florida and Julia. Then he located his beloved cat, Gato, took his book satchel, and went into the hidden room to do his homework. He had set up a little desk. He had a small picture of St. Michael which Father had given him on his baptism day. This he pinned to the wall.

Julia had believed that he would never want to enter the room again after the events of that terrible day when Beast came to kidnap him, but the opposite had proved to be the case. The little room was his special safe place. Jon Teel held firm to his belief that his mother had joined forces with Michael the archangel to force the hidden door open in the stairway, tripping Beast and causing his downfall. One day, Julia asked him about it.

"Jon, you know you don't have to hide away to do your homework. You could sit right here in the kitchen where Florida and I can help you if the need arises."

"Mama J, don't worry when I go in my little room. It's my thinking place. It's where I talk to Mami and my *abuelos*. They're all happy in a beautiful place."

Again, Julia was taken aback by the child's apparent belief that he was communing with his dead mother and his relatives who were God-knew-where in Mexico. Julia decided there was no harm in his spending time alone in the little room after school each day. Occasionally, she heard his voice as she passed the hidden door in the wainscoting in the hall as though he were carrying on a one-sided conversation with someone.

Julia had made good on her promise to seek counseling for Jon Teel. One afternoon each week, she drove him to New Iberia for a session with the child psychologists.

Sometimes, it was the wife and sometimes the husband of the duo who met with the boy. They too were puzzled by his matter-of-fact acceptance of all that had happened to him including the awful death of his mother.

"He has such faith that she is in a better place and that she is looking out for him. We've never come across a case quite like Jon Teel's, but we both agree that he is in a good place. If this little bit of fantasy helps him exist and even thrive, we see no harm," they reported to Julia, recommending that his visits be changed from weekly to monthly, simply to monitor his progress.

Oddly, Jon Teel began to take special notice of school busses that passed them as they walked home from school each afternoon.

"Abuelita will ride on such a bus," he commented one day.

"What makes you say that, Jon?" Julia asked.

"She told me in my dreams," he replied matter-of-factly.

*****

Julia decided it was time to meet with Sheriff Joe Blanchard to ascertain that he had his feelers out for information on Jon Teel's relatives who might be alive in Mexico.

"Julia," Sheriff Blanchard began when he answered Julia's telephone call, "I've had dreadful news from the police chief in Laredo who heard it from the chief in Saltillo, Mexico. Apparently, the remnants of Jonathan Steelman's gang have turned into a cult worshiping a dark goddess called Santa Muerte, literally the face of death. They claim that she drives them to do unspeakable acts in her name. The news I received is that they hunted down Jon Teel's mother's family and burned them alive, first the children as the parents watched and then the parents themselves. Jon Teel's mother was sold into that gang to save her family, but it served no purpose except to get her family killed in the cruelest way. I understand the story has been picked up by national news agencies here in the states."

Julia felt that she might be sick. She took a breath and recovered.

"This is the most dreadful news," she said, "but, Joe, if her father hadn't sold Maria Maristella to Jonathan Steelman, we wouldn't have Jon Teel."

"Another bit of news is that Samuel Burleson and Jonathan Steelman have been extradited to Texas to stand trial. The Louisiana attorney general decided that the murder over in Houston took precedence over the attempted kidnapping and assault in Louisiana. The fact that the boy is Steelman's biological son muddied the waters on the attempted kidnapping charge. They are wanted for other murders in Texas. Word gets around in prisons. The way they treated Maria Maristella and her family, and given the large population of prisoners of Hispanic descent incarcerated in Texas, I don't expect them to fare very well."

Julia tried to decide whether or not she should tell Jon Teel the horrifying news about his grandparents and his young aunts and uncles and their gruesome murders. When she met him at St. John later that day for their walk home, she decided she had to tell him something. If the Lafayette television station picked up the story and made the connection to Maria Maristella and Jon Teel, it was only a matter of time before someone said something to the boy.

"Jon," Julia began, her voice catching as she tried to find the words, "something very bad has happened."

"It's okay, Mama J. Mami told me in my dream last night. It was very terrible, and my grandparents and Mami's sisters and brothers hurt a lot. But it ended fast, and they are together with Mami in a place so beautiful I don't have the words. And Mami told me not to worry. Great-grandmother, Abuelita, is coming. She'll soon be on her way. Will you let her live with us, Mama J?"

Julia continued to walk in stunned silence. Jon Teel must have overheard someone talking about the mass murder of his family in Mexico. His calm acceptance floored Julia. If this truly was the boy's martyred mother's intervention and she really was communing with the boy, she was most certainly a viable candidate for sainthood.

"Of course, your great-grandmother can live with us. She can live with us forever, Jon Teel," Julia finally replied.

SALTILLO

At his makeshift home in the little gorge, Juan Diego sat on a small stool drinking a cup of coffee that he made on his adobe brick stove. He survived on very little in the way of purchased food. He bought masa to make tortillas; he bought dried beans and a little lard, but otherwise, he foraged fruit and vegetables from the nearby farms and orchards.

This morning, he was holding a piece of cherry wood deciding what to make of it. He was a talented wood carver, using only his old pocketknife. He used whatever wood he found around his place, but he found that the small local cedars and the rare cherry trees produced the wood best suited to his carving style.

Cherry trees weren't common in the area, but there were four growing well in a nearby fruit orchard. The caretaker pruned them periodically, stacking the wood along the perimeter of the orchard. Juan Diego was free to help himself. Mostly, he carved simple animals, but sometimes, he attempted religious figures. He painted most of his carvings, but some of them, particularly the animals, he left in their natural state, especially if the wood had a distinctive grain or pattern. He had amassed an impressive collection of figures for his modest Day of the Dead altar. He was especially proud of the grotesque images of skulls and skeletons which challenged his carving skill. He decided that the piece of cherry wood that he held would be suited to the shape of a small sacred heart with flames coming out of the top. This was one of his favorite carving motifs. He made a tentative cut, the wood responding nicely to his skilled knife.

Then he set the wood carving aside deciding he had more pressing matters on his agenda. He decided to eat the last of the bread rolls from the bishop. His plan was taking shape. He had been reading a page daily from the little Bible the bishop had given him. Juan Diego could read, albeit painstakingly. The biblical language was difficult, but he made himself do it at first light every morning. He found that the practice was giving him insight and ideas into the course of action he should follow. Genesis, in the beginning. The tiny mustard seed that became a tree that was home to many birds. Even God had to start somewhere. Juan Diego would start with the bus, and when he had it presentable enough, he would show it to the bishop.

The bus was the key to his whole plan for saving the grandmother of Maria Maristella, but he would need the bishop on board, at least in spirit. There were official channels to navigate. Only a person with the power of the bishop could get the necessary legal documents that Juan Diego assumed would be required for the bus. He had to tread carefully.

In the early morning light, he took out the little statue from the cathedral trash and considered what he must do to bring her back to life. The small chips were easy. The face was the critical part. He felt a direct connection to heaven whenever he painted the eyes on a statue. They were a true window to the soul, and he believed the personage represented by the statue could see directly into his own soul.

Juan Diego and Jon Teel, although they had never met, had a spiritual kinship: the lines between the spiritual and concrete reality seemed to be blurred for them. The spiritual was very much a part of their everyday lives. Jon Teel communed daily with his dead mother, his grandparents, and Michael the archangel. Juan Diego conversed with the Virgin of Guadalupe as though she were walking along with him as he led Bonita on their rounds.

Juan Diego had decided that the small statue would be his gift to the bishop. He would do his very best work— demonstrating for the bishop his capabilities as a craftsman and artist—before he worked up the courage to broach the subject of his grand plan for the school bus.

His paints were poor quality, leftovers from here and there, but he required only small amounts. He took his time, especially with her beautiful face. This image was what Juan Diego considered to be a "good" statue. Many such religious artifacts were not good quality, having ugly, crude facial features. The best paints couldn't fix that. This little statue of the Virgin had delicate features, an exquisite small nose, and lovely eyes. Juan Diego's talent was such that a few brushstrokes applied with exactness would make her better than new. He knew innately the adage "less is more."

He spoke to the small plaster figure as he worked, outlining his dream of saving the old grandmother by taking her on the bus to join her great-grandson in Louisiana. He called her "Little Lupe" as he told her how much he needed her help. He worked slowly with a sure hand. When he finished, he set her on the brick stove, near his small fire, so that the paint would dry and cure. Then he walked over to the bus and examined it for the hundredth time. It was at least thirty years old, made by the Blue Bird Bus Corporation in the state of Georgia in the United States of America.

The interior of the bus was immaculate. Someone had lovingly reupholstered all the seats. The tires were far from new, but they had a respectable amount of tread depth left

on them. All this Juan Diego was capable of assessing. He knew that the bus started with reassuring regularity on the first try every single time. He turned the ignition and ran it for a minute or two each week. It had a nearly full gas tank, but he didn't want to use the fuel up needlessly. The time would come when he would need it. He kept the large envelope of papers that came with the bus in their secure hiding place.

When he opened the engine compartment, he was completely out of his element. He could readily see that the engine was clean, the battery connections not corroded. He suspected that this engine was a replacement, not the original one from the factory. He would need the help of a skilled mechanic to assess the current state of health of the bus's working parts. Again, his mind focused on the bishop as the answer to his needs. But how to be certain that the bishop could maintain secrecy?

Juan Diego retrieved Bonita from the patch of good green grass where he had staked her.

"Let's go see our friend, the bishop, my pretty girl," he murmured. "It's Monday morning, and he will be expecting us."

He was filled with a gratifying warmth that a man such as the bishop would be looking forward to a visit from the likes of him. Juan Diego and Bonita ambled along at a moderate pace, going along the side of the big highway. They made their way into the city of Saltillo, to the heart of the town. They turned the corner and entered the back alley behind the cathedral. Juan Diego patted his pocket containing the refurbished statue that he planned to give to the bishop. He glanced up at the bishop's study window and gave a tiny wave.

The bishop, anticipating the arrival of the man and his donkey cart, watched as they entered the alleyway. The rising sun sent a shaft of bright light down onto the man and the donkey, enveloping them in a heavenly aura. The bishop took in the scene then motioned for Juan Diego to enter the courtyard. Once inside, Juan Diego tethered Bonita near the water barrel and let himself inside the back entrance. Seeing no one, he took the liberty of climbing the stairs and knocking on the bishop's study door.

"Enter," the bishop's distinctive voice came through the heavy paneled wood door.

Juan Diego entered, his straw hat in his hand. He made a point of standing straight and tall or as tall as his short stature allowed. He reached into his pocket and drew out the statue he had repainted, offering it to the bishop without a word.

The bishop's eyes widened in amazement. The little statue was very beautiful, delicate, painted with obvious mastery. Based on this sample of his work, the bishop would not have hesitated to allow this unassuming little fellow to work on the finest statuary in the cathedral. But the man's artistic talent was not foremost in the bishop's thoughts this Monday morning.

"You are a very talented man, sir," the bishop said, "but please keep the little Virgin. She can be your protector and your talisman as we take this journey together. I trust you have news for me?"

Juan Diego had already decided not to play his hand just yet. He wanted to try to learn just how much help he might expect from the bishop before he told him anything concrete. Also, he had a plan for assuring the bishop's secrecy.

"I have some leads, your excellency, but nothing definite just yet. Give me another week, and I should have good information. But tell me, sir, how do you plan to proceed if you find the grandmother of Maria Maristella?"

"A good question, my friend. I understand that you don't want to do anything that would jeopardize the safety of the old woman knowing what we do about the fate of the rest of her family. So first and foremost, I will assure her physical safety by whatever means necessary. I won't involve the police or the authorities in any manner. There are too many who would betray the poor woman for money. My plan is to get word to the bishop in the diocese in Louisiana through official church mail—which should be very safe—and try to seek asylum for her there where she can be reunited with her grandson. I'll do all of this through official channels as I work to begin proving that Maria Maristella is worthy of sainthood. I want that information to become public knowledge. That may give the drug cartel scoundrels pause and stop them from seeking to torment the poor family any further or what is left of the family."

Juan Diego listened attentively to the long speech, approving of what he heard. The bishop's thinking paralleled his own thoughts about how best to save the little grandmother. He spoke up.

"Bishop, what is required for sainthood?"

"We already have definite proof that the girl died a cruel death, murdered because she refused to reveal the whereabouts of her child. That is undisputed, with proof, in the hands of the forensic laboratory in the capital of Louisiana and in the words of the monster who tortured and murdered her.

Next, there must be a miracle definitely attributable to Maria Maristella. Reports of such miracles have been pouring in. The faithful all over Mexico are praying to the young girl to intercede for them. There have been reports of cancer cures, paralytics walking, all sorts of wonderful happenings. But reports are one thing and undisputed proof is another. This all takes time. But unless we begin, it will never happen. I firmly believe in her cause, and I will work with every fiber of my being to prove it. If I must go to Rome on the girl's behalf, I will go."

Juan Diego was in awe of this good man and vowed that he would take him into his confidence but all in good time. He had a bit more work to do, and he also wanted the permission of the little grandmother before he revealed her whereabouts and his plan to save her. He took his leave of the bishop and returned to his home to go to work on the bus. The bus was the keystone of his developing plan.

After much consideration, he had decided to keep the yellow paint which had been refurbished and was in fair condition. There was a reason for the yellow color on school busses, he reasoned. It had to be quite visible and therefore safer than a more pleasing but bland color. His vision was to make the bus as bright and noticeable as he could. He intended to drive it all the way to Louisiana. His goal was not to hide from the bad guys but to make such a spectacle that they would not be able to interfere. He also wanted to distract attention from the precious cargo he planned to hide inside the bus: the grandmother of soon-to-be-saint Maria Maristella. He didn't dwell too much on the ramifications of his ambitious plan, or he might have given up before he started.

He worked steadily on the bus for many days, forgoing his trips into town. He made adornments to attach to the sides of the vehicle. He had a cache of thin flat metal scraps from old, discarded signs he had found here and there. These he cut into large shapes resembling the small metal milagros the faithful attached to the statues in church. Using old tinsnips and a hacksaw, he painstakingly cut out the shapes of hearts, eyes, arms, legs, and several pairs of angel wings.

He dragged out a heavy piece of flat iron that served as his anvil. Next, he located a big hammer. He began to beat the tin pieces into the shapes he thought they should be. He found himself thinking of the cruel people who had murdered Maria Maristella and began to beat the metal harder and harder, his anger rising with each blow. Suddenly, he set the hammer down and took a deep breath.

"Lord God," he prayed aloud, "turn my anger to do your will. Make me a strong hammer to fight like the archangels for good. Let me be the hammer, not the anvil." He didn't realize that he echoed the words of St. Dominic.

He picked up the hammer once more, but this time he beat the metal with hard, rhythmic strokes, firm but not angry. Using the silver paint left in the near-empty cans that he had scavenged, he painted the cut-out forms silver. He cut out two large crosses which he painted bright metallic gold. These he planned to attach to the front and the back of the bus. He stacked all the finished metal forms safely in his workshop while he went to work on the outside of the bus.

Humming as he labored, standing on a crude wooden ladder, he drew large, exuberant scrolling vines with leaves all over the sides of the bus. He painted all of it in shades of green. Then he painted large, happy flowers in red, blue, orange, and purple. The people would see his bus coming a mile away. Using old metal screws, he attached the silver milagros all over the bus. He was pleased with the way they shone in the sunlight. Finally, he put the gold crosses on the front and the back. He painted over the Tabernacle Church lettering, writing in big letters on both sides of the bus, "The Miracle Bus—Sainthood for Maria Maristella."

All this hard work took nearly two weeks, with Juan Diego laboring from dawn until dark each day, stopping only to eat small scraps of food. Finally, he was ready to reveal his plan to the bishop. First though, he must make a visit to the campsite where the grandmother of Maria Maristella was hidden.

*****

During the time that Juan Diego was refurbishing and adorning the bus, the bishop was fretting. Why had he not figured out a way to contact Juan Diego? He had no physical address for the man and certainly no telephone. What if he never heard from him again? The bishop had gotten the distinct impression that Juan Diego had information but that he was not ready or willing to share it. Juan Diego had mentioned that he lived in the countryside south of the city of Saltillo, but that covered a great deal of territory. The only choice the bishop had was to wait, and that was not in his nature. He was a man of action. He called Father Fernando into his office to deal with the mundane business matters of the day. He decided to initiate the paperwork to begin the process of sainthood for young Maria Maristella.

This would be an ambitious project. The process of submitting an applicant for sainthood generally began in the diocese in which the person died. The bishop decided that this application should come from three bishops working together: the bishop of the Archdiocese of Houston-Galveston where Maria Maristella was murdered, the bishop of the Diocese of Lafayette in Louisiana where she had delivered her young son, and himself, the bishop in Saltillo, Mexico, birthplace of the girl. There was, he reasoned, strength in numbers.

Any bishop should be delighted to welcome a new saint. Besides the obvious spiritual benefits, a new saint of local interest tended to bring people back into the church. It was, simply put, good PR. The bishop was a practical man. He knew that attendance at Mass was dwindling. St. Maria Maristella could help bring the wayward back into the fold.

He also thought sainthood for Maria Maristella could prove to be powerful ammunition against the drug cartels and their cult of death. The process for obtaining sainthood generally did not begin until five years after the death of the candidate, but the bishop felt that the Pope might be persuaded to shorten the period in the case of the young martyr killed by the drug cartel. He would like to have definitive proof of her good character. Her missing relatives might provide that or her former teachers or even the jailed criminals who had held her captive. He would work on all that. Certainly, she had no written works of a spiritual nature. The only items that he knew of that were written in her hand were the notes tucked into the old books she sent to Louisiana with her son. Those painstakingly written notes had brought down a gang of drug dealers.

The bishop was deeply concerned for the young people of his diocese, especially young men, who were drawn into the cartels, lured by easy money, automatic weapons, and a seemingly glamourous life. For most of them, that life ended at a very early age.

"Such a waste," the bishop often sighed.

He viewed sainthood for Maria Maristella as a great weapon against the cartels and their devotion to Santa Muerte. Sainthood for Maria Maristella would be a defeat for the cult of death. Though she was physically dead, she would live on in the most beautiful way.

The bishop thought about the next steps to proceed with the application for sainthood as he prayed his daily rosary. He was a great devotee of the holy rosary. Today, it was the sorrowful mysteries. Of all the twenty mysteries of the rosary, his favorites were "the nativity" and "the carrying of the cross." The nativity mystery commemorated the birth of the tiny baby Jesus who changed the world. The carrying of the cross could be applied to every single human who ever lived. Everyone had a cross to bear. If one did not have any problems, that only meant they had not yet arrived. Some of his parishioners had terrible crosses: badly disabled children, incurable cancers, parents with dementia. An endless list of afflictions plagued the human race. The bishop tried, in his weekly homilies, to give his flock the strength and vision to see these trials as bricks paving the way to heaven and not as punishment. It was a tough assignment.

He decided that he would approach the archbishop of Houston-Galveston in an official letter. He would send a copy to the bishop in Lafayette, Louisiana. He called Father Fernando into his study and began dictating.

*****

Juan Diego made his way down to the encampment to see the little grandmother of Maria Maristella. He greeted her with respect then asked her if she would like to be reunited with her great-grandson in Louisiana. She nodded a definite affirmative, her eyes shining.

"Then I would like to ask you to come with me to see what I think will make it possible."

With several members of the encampment tagging along, Juan Diego led the woman down to his home. He led them behind his workshop where the bus was hidden. He removed the tattered tarps that covered it revealing the brilliantly decorated vehicle. The group stood in amazed silence. Juan Diego turned to Abuelita.

"With the help of God and the bishop, I intend to drive you to Louisiana!"

The group readily gave Juan Diego permission to let the bishop in on the location of their hideout. Every single one of them hoped to go on the ambitious journey. They would be pilgrims helping to set Abuelita free.

There was one more thing Juan Diego wanted to do. He went to the orchard woodpile and selected a small scrap of cherry wood. He took it back to his workshop, turned it this way and that, and began to carve. With a few cuts of his knife, he made an uncanny little replica of the bus. It was his special wooden version of a milagro made with love from his heart.

The following Saturday, nearly two weeks after his last meeting with the bishop, Juan Diego went to cathedral. He went to an alcove that housed a statue of the Blessed Mother. There, he placed his carved wooden bus milagro. He knelt before the statue for a long time, offering prayers of petition for the success of his grand plan.

Then he went to sit in a back corner of the cathedral, intently watching the confessional. He knew that the bishop was hearing confessions. Every time the line dwindled, Juan Diego got up to get at the end of it. Several times, another penitent showed up and got in line behind him. Each time, Juan Diego went back to his pew to wait.

His thoughts were far away from recounting his sins. He was planning the words that he would say to the bishop. Finally, the last person left the confessional, walking to the front of the cathedral to recite the prayers he had been given as a penance. Juan Diego slipped into the dark cubicle.

"Bless me, Excellency, I am a sinner. It is I, Juan Diego. I have news. I give it to you in the confessional to seal the secret between us. I have the information you seek."

The bishop sat back in his chair as though he had received an electric shock.

What a curious, intelligent little man, he thought, *using the seal of confession to assure my silence.*

"My friend, you appear to be the last penitent. Don't say another word. Even the walls of the cathedral aren't safe. First though, because I know you are a good man, I absolve you from any sins you may have. Recite an Act of Contrition, then go to the front of the cathedral and say three Our Fathers and three Hail Marys, then return to your home. I want to give you my full attention when we discuss this matter. Let me get through the weekend masses. Come on Monday morning as you always do. That won't attract any attention. Come up to my study. There, our conversation will be safe. And rest assured that I will consider it to be under the seal of the confessional.

BAKERVILLE

Life in Bakerville had taken on an easy routine. Jon Teel enjoyed his days at St. John. He had made friends. He had regular playdates with classmates who accompanied him home after school. His grades were excellent, and his appetite was good. He continued to spend time in the hidden room, occasionally reporting on conversations he had with his dead mother.

Julia had fulfilled most of the items on the to-do list she had made in the hospital. The two New Iberia psychologists gave Jon Teel excellent reports each month. All was good.

Judge Porteus Green reported that the adoption documents for Jon Teel were complete and ironclad. The child's mother was dead, and his father was in jail for orchestrating her murder. Jonathan Steelman's parental rights had been legally severed by the court with no problem. Julia and Jon Teel appeared before the judge. Jon Teel emphatically expressed his desire to be adopted by Julia, and the adoption was processed.

On a Wednesday morning, the pastor called from the rectory.

"Julia, I've had an unusual call from the chancery office in Lafayette. The bishop is coming to meet with me tomorrow. He has requested your presence at the meeting. I have no idea what it's about, but I can only assume it has to do with Jon Teel and his mother. I can't think of any other reason. You know, there is a cultlike worship of Jon Teel's mother growing daily in and around her hometown of Saltillo in northern Mexico. There's even talk of sainthood for her. I can't think of any reason for this meeting except to discuss something about your boy's mother. Anyway, if you can be here at ten in the morning, I would appreciate it."

Julia presented herself at the rectory a few minutes before ten the next morning. Over coffee in the pleasant rectory kitchen, she and the pastor discussed what might be behind the mysterious visit. Julia expected the bishop to roll up to the front door in a limousine. Instead, precisely at ten, he drove himself in his white Toyota Camry under the carport behind the rectory and let himself in the back door.

"Wonderful! You have the coffee pot on. I'll help myself to a cup and fill you in on the purpose of my visit. I'm sure you're brimming with curiosity."

He got his coffee, choosing a big mug and filling it full then adding cream and sugar. He joined them at the table.

"Mrs. Hancock, I believe we met some years ago when you received an award at our annual Mass."

Julia was pleased that he remembered.

"My visit today concerns your adopted son, the child of the murdered girl Maria Maristella Lopez. She is causing quite the stir in her native Mexico, particularly in and around her birthplace, which is the city of Saltillo. The bishop there has asked me to join him and the archbishop of Houston-Galveston in petitioning for sainthood for the young woman. I have agreed. Generally, such action isn't taken until five years after the death of the candidate. The bishop in Saltillo feels, and I believe rightly so, that the girl's cruel death in saving her boy was certainly martyrdom. He further believes that pushing forward with sainthood for the girl will send a message and serve as a blow to the drug cartels and their death cult. I'm inclined to agree with him on this as well. We've all seen the destruction caused by the influx of drugs into our state. The Houston archbishop is also in agreement."

Julia and Father sat in stunned silence. They had often said that Maria Maristella ought to be a saint. However, hearing the words from the bishop took it to a much higher level.

"Which brings me to the immediate reason for my visit today. Mrs. Hancock, I understand that the responsibility for the remains of the murdered girl has fallen upon your shoulders. Her family has been murdered; the awful man who did all these despicable deeds and fathered her child never married Maria Maristella, and you have officially adopted her son. It appears to be left to you to decide upon a final resting place for young Maria. What is your plan for the remains of Maria Maristella once they are released by the forensics lab in Baton Rouge?"

"I plan to have her interred in our family plot with an appropriate granite marker," Julia stammered.

"May I make a strong new suggestion? There has been an exploding interest in and devotion to young Maria in northern Mexico. I feel certain that it will find its way here, to your town, especially when it becomes known that she is buried here. My proposal is that the diocese help fund the building of a modest, very secure mausoleum here on the church grounds. There are already several persons of importance to the parish interred in the fenced churchyard next to the church building. This will be a more fitting burial site, readily accessible to you and your son for visitation, and more appropriate for her remains should she attain sainthood. In that eventuality, those remains would become sacred relics.

"Frankly, I don't think her grave would be safe in the unattended Bakerville cemetery. Of course, people visit the grave of young Charlene Richard, which is in the diocese. It's in a small country cemetery, and there have been no problems. However, Maria Maristella, with her gruesome murder and connection to the drug cartel, might be an entirely different matter."

Julia was astounded. The pastor was also taken aback. They digested the bishop's request in stunned silence. The pastor spoke first.

"I'm certainly agreeable with having a possible future saint buried in our churchyard, but it's really up to Mrs. Julia."

"You have caught me completely off guard, your excellency, but of course, I'll abide by your wishes. I can certainly pay whatever cost there is. I don't want the diocese to have to foot the bill for it."

"The diocese is happy to pay all or part of the cost. We will have some very specific design requests that I hope will be agreeable with you, Mrs. Hancock. I already have someone working on it in the hope that you would be amenable. We will have an appropriate funeral when the time comes. I plan to come to concelebrate the service with your pastor. The archbishop may come from Houston if he is able. The bishop in Saltillo requested that we wait awhile

on the funeral. He has some new leads and is hoping to locate Maria Maristella's only remaining close relative: her maternal grandmother. He's hoping to move her safely to Louisiana and gain asylum for her. He asked that we keep this in utmost secrecy because she has a huge target on her back in Mexico, poor creature. Her whole family has been murdered except for her great-grandson, your adopted child, Mrs. Hancock."

This was an astounding information for Julia to process. She decided to go along with the bishop whom she admired.

"Your excellency, whatever design you come up with for the mausoleum will be fine with me. Jon Teel continues to say that his mother tells him in dreams that his *abuelita*—his great-grandmother—is coming. He is a very spiritual child. He says she's coming on a school bus. I don't know what to make of it."

"I don't know about the bus part, Mrs. Hancock, but let's hope his prophecy comes true and his great-grandmother can somehow be spirited out of Mexico and come here to Bakerville to be reunited with her great-grandson," the bishop said.

"She will always have a home with me," Julia said.

Julia reported the gist of the meeting to Jon Teel. He smiled and nodded as though she were only affirming information he already knew.

SALTILLO

The area near Juan Diego's modest home was dotted with small *fincas*—little farms owned by wealthy city people who visited them during summer months to enjoy the cooler climate at the higher altitude. There were fruit orchards and nice pastures. Juan Diego sometimes took the liberty of tethering Bonita in a nearby pasture attached to one of these small farms. The owner had given permission, liking the idea that the donkey could help keep the grass clipped. Bonita enjoyed the verdant pasture. The owner also appreciated the occasional presence of Juan Diego on the property to give the appearance that it was occupied.

*****

At first light on Monday morning, Juan Diego led Bonita to the pasture and tethered her there on a long rope. She had access to a water trough and could rest in the shade of a small tree. After telling her goodbye, he set off walking to Saltillo. He never felt daunted by the long walk, enjoying the time to sort out his many thoughts and dreams. When he arrived at the cathedral, he let himself into the back door of the bishop's residence and went up the stairs to knock on the door of the bishop's study. Father

Fernando answered the door as the bishop was on a telephone call with the pastor of a particularly difficult parish.

"Good morning," Father Fernando said pleasantly, "Is the bishop expecting you?"

"Yes, Father," Juan Diego replied, "he told me to come."

"Then you must wait in the hallway until he completes his business on the telephone."

He shut the door, leaving Juan Diego to stand in the hall. After a few minutes, both the bishop and Father Fernando came to the door. The bishop spoke.

"Ah, my friend, I am so sorry. Father Fernando should have offered you coffee. Father Fernando, please fetch coffee for me and for my friend. Lots of sugar and cream."

Father Fernando, impassive as always, departed, closing the door behind him.

*****

Father Fernando Flores, the bishop's right-hand man, had known from boyhood that he wanted to be a priest. The mother of six sons, Fernando's mother happily accepted her young son's chosen vocation. He attended parochial school where he earned respectable grades but was not a shining star. He was a steadfast student, average, always earning perfect attendance. He was devout, exhibiting signs of deep faith at an early age. The principal of the school assured his parents that the seminary would welcome him. As soon as he reached the minimum age, he entered to study for the priesthood. He never wavered or doubted his decision to become a Roman Catholic priest.

When he completed his studies, he served as an assistant pastor in the cathedral parish where his strong sense of duty attracted the attention of the bishop who was seeking a secretary. This was a great honor in the eyes of Father Fernando and his family. He readily accepted, although the offer was more of a command than a request. He soon proved his worth to the bishop, fulfilling all his duties with a cheerful attitude and a minimum of fuss. He understood the bishop's need to help the poor, the disenfranchised, the underpaid workers of his diocese. He watched as the bishop met with representatives of these groups of people.

Father Fernando could accept what he could see and understand, but he was a man of little imagination. When the bishop began having secret meetings with the odd Indian man, Father Fernando was puzzled and out of his depth. Using what little imagination he had, he tried to envision scenarios that would require such meetings. Was the bishop searching for some odd object that the man might come across in his foraging expeditions? Father Fernando had caught a glimpse of the little statue the man had refurbished. Could the bishop have an artistic project in mind?

The bishop had a large group of skilled artists and artisans who regularly maintained the many statues and artworks in the cathedral, so that shouldn't be the reason. There was no one he could ask because it was an unspoken rule that the business dealings of the bishop to which Father Fernando was privy were to be held in strict confidence. Father Fernando decided to bide his time and wait for an opportunity to ask the bishop directly what was going on with Juan Diego. The bishop's obvious deference to the man this morning, having Father Fernando fetch him coffee, had his interest piqued more than ever. He would await an opportunity and he would ask. Surely, the bishop owed him some sort of explanation.

While Father Fernando was out of the room, the bishop began.

"Now, my friend, what is so urgent and so secret that you must resort to the seal of the confessional? Don't you believe that you can trust me?"

"Of course, Excellency, but you must understand. The life of an innocent woman is in our hands. I know where the grandmother of Maria Maristella is hiding. She is safe for the moment, but the location is far from secure. We must act quickly to get her out of this country. I have a plan, but you may think my plan is crazy."

The bishop thought he had heard everything, but when Juan Diego related the tale of the runaway bus, the dead driver, the disappearing passenger that he thought was St. Raphael, the archangel, he had trouble taking it all in. He decided to tackle one item at a time, beginning with the bus.

"So this school bus, the one with the dead driver, is it still at the place in the country where you make your home?"

"Yes, Excellency, I have it well-hidden. I have decorated it to the best of my ability for the trip to Louisiana. I have named it "The Miracle Bus." I expect to make the trip in one day, traveling at fifty-five miles per hour. It will be a long day, but I can do it. The bus appears to be in good condition for its age. The tires aren't great, but they should make it for the 650 miles there and 650 miles back. I plan to hide the little grandmother on the bus. We will be pilgrims going to promote canonization for Maria Maristella and hoping to meet her young son. With your official blessing, it's the perfect disguise for the grandmother of our beloved Maria Maristella. But her grandmother won't ride with the passengers any time that she might be seen. I have a plan to hide her quite safely on the bus. It's my belief

that if we make a big spectacle, call a lot of attention to the bus and our pilgrimage, we can spirit the old grandmother away without arousing suspicion. But I need some things from you."

The bishop went to his desk chair and sat down. He folded his hands together in a prayerful manner, his thinking pose. He frowned. He wrinkled his brow. Finally, he broke out in a big smile.

"My friend, I think it just might work. What do you need? And remember, you still have not revealed the location of the grandmother. However, if you know where she is, perhaps, for the moment, I don't even need to know."

At that moment, Father Fernando entered the study bearing a tray with three steaming pottery mugs of strong coffee. He had taken the liberty of fixing one for himself in the hope that he might join in the conversation. He set the tray down on the bishop's desk, handing one mug to the bishop and a second one to Juan Diego. The bishop did not disappoint his eager young assistant.

"Juan Diego, I must ask your permission to let Father Fernando in on our secret. He is completely trustworthy. He is a great believer in the cause of sainthood for Maria Maristella Lopez. I can't go out into the countryside to see your project and help you with it. I can't accompany you to Louisiana, but I would like to have Father Fernando go along with you. He can be the spiritual director and chaplain. In addition, he will give a great deal of credence to the idea that the bus is carrying a load of pilgrims to walk in the steps of Maria Maristella. I like it! I like it! Do I have your permission to include him in our plan?"

The bishop was already calling it "our plan," which made Juan Diego's heart sing. He had expected to have to plead his case at length. He offered a quick prayer of thanksgiving and readily agreed. Father Fernando was coming aboard the Miracle Bus. Father Fernando, for his part, was shocked to his core by the revelation that all the secrecy he had witnessed surrounded Maria Maristella and the saving of her aged grandmother. He needed no convincing. So certain was he that Maria would be recognized as a saint that he would have staked his life on it. If he traveled on the Miracle Bus, he might have to do just that.

The bishop was already making plans.

"Fernando, get a notepad and make written notes which you will keep under lock and key. Nothing on your computer or iPad. I want no trail that the internet might pick up. First, I intend to publicize the plans I have to work toward sainthood for this special girl. Write down as number 1, 'Call the editor of *El Diario*.' The editor is a parishioner. He comes to Mass only for Christmas and Easter, but he'll be happy to have this headline. I plan to tell him that

I am hoping that two other bishops will join me in requesting that the five-year requirement be set aside for young Maria and that the process for sainthood will begin as soon as possible. Then I intend to tell him that the Diocese of Saltillo is sending a group of pilgrims to Louisiana to promote the cause for Maria Maristella's sainthood."

Juan Diego's mouth hung open a bit as he listened to the bishop outlining the best way to bring his plan to life. He looked upward toward heaven and voiced a silent prayer of thanksgiving. The bishop was putting Juan Diego's thoughts and dreams into succinct words.

"The best way to spirit the grandmother of Maria Maristella out of the country and out of reach of those who would kill her is to make a big fanfare. We'll call all the attention to the bus that we can drum up. We'll have people lining the streets along the way. We'll print up cards with pictures of young Maria and ask for donations for this worthy cause. Why, I'll even dedicate a second collection to help pay for the trip. We'll get you a new set of tires for that bus!"

Father Fernando was writing furiously.

"Next, write down for number 2, 'Call Sancho Ramirez at his garage and tell him I have a special project that will take care of his donations to the church for the whole year and that his garage can be listed as an official sponsor of the

Miracle Bus that will go to the United States promoting the cause of canonization for Maria Maristella Lopez. Ramirez loves the spotlight. He'll be onboard without any need for begging. I want the bus in tip-top shape for the trip."

The bishop paused for breath, took a big sip of coffee, and made a comment, as though thinking out loud.

"The Holy Father won't appreciate my public campaign for sainthood. No, he won't like it at all. Perhaps at the next meeting I have with him in Rome, I'll have the opportunity to explain the special circumstances. I do truly believe all this fanfare and attention focused on the bus will be our best chance of getting Maria Maristella's grandmother out of danger of murder at the hands of the cartels. I also think an early canonization of the girl will be a huge weapon against the cartels and their sick, heretical worship of Santa Muerte."

Father Fernando's heart was pounding. In his wildest dreams, he had never expected to be a part of something this big and this meaningful. His mother would be so proud! The bishop dashed any hope he had of sharing the news with his next statement.

"Finally, the three of us must swear a solemn oath never to reveal the true purpose of the trip of the Miracle Bus. Father Fernando, you may share with your family that you are my official ambassador and representative. You may tell

them you are going on the pilgrimage as chaplain and spiritual director. Juan Diego, you have my permission to invite all the people who are living with the grandmother and keeping her safe. How many of them do you expect to make the pilgrimage?"

Juan Diego counted on his fingers.

"Seven, your excellency."

"And how many can we safely send without overcrowding the bus? Twenty?"

"Twenty would be a good number, your excellency."

"Fine. I will carefully choose thirteen parishioners that I know can be trusted. They won't know of the secret passenger until the bus is underway. We will require that all cellphones be turned off and given to Father Fernando for safekeeping until the bus crosses over into the United States. We can't have any secret text messages or telephone calls no matter how well-intentioned. Anyone who won't comply will be escorted off the bus. Now then, tell me how you plan to hide the woman on a small school bus? What will you need?"

Juan Diego smiled angelically.

"All I need, your Excellency, is a small coffin."

BAKERVILLE

Within a week, excavating equipment appeared in the churchyard to prepare the ground for the mausoleum. Jimmie Daniel II of Daniel Granite, the leading maker of tombs and markers in the area, assured the pastor that they were more than capable and ready to take on the task of building the mausoleum as soon as the chancery office sent them the plans and specifications. The strong metal door and secure locking mechanism that the bishop required were not a problem. They would order the very best. It would be expensive, but they would do the work for the best possible price. They wouldn't charge for their services, only for the required materials.

Damon Robicheaux of Robicheaux Heating and Cooling submitted plans for the best climate control system for their purposes. It would maintain a constant optimum temperature and humidity year-round. This was one of the must-have items on the bishop's list. He planned to consult with and work with Jimmie Daniel as the mausoleum was constructed.

After the ground was prepared and soil samples checked, Baldwin Readi-Mix arrived with a churning load of concrete and poured the slab on which the mausoleum would be built. They too donated their services. At this rate, the final resting place of Maria Marisella Lopez would soon be ready.

Scott Pellerin from Ibert's Mortuary consulted with the chancery office on a proper casket for the remains. It had to be the highest quality, completely sealed for the interment but able to be reopened with ease should the need arise. Ibert's would also be involved in discreetly retrieving the remains of Maria Maristella from the forensics lab in Baton Rouge for transport to Bakerville when the time came. Scott Pellerin intended to take care of it himself.

Julia and Jon Teel stopped by each afternoon on their way back from St. John Elementary to oversee the work on the mausoleum. As Julia monitored the progress and the cooperation among all the talented people involved in the building of Maria Maristella's final resting place, she was filled with pride that she could count them among her friends. Bakerville was fortunate to have them.

Jon Teel spoke of the large tomb as though it were a home being constructed where his mother would take up residence, not the place where her remains would be interred.

SALTILLO

Juan Diego was ready with an explanation when the bishop asked about the need for a coffin.

"Your Excellency, the coffin is the key to the whole plan. I will remove rows of seats at the rear of the bus and build a wooden platform. The platform will have a door in front, but the door will be concealed. The coffin will go on top of the wooden platform. It will be decorated beautifully to contain a life-size mannequin representing Maria Maristella Lopez. She will be dressed appropriately, maybe in white like on her confirmation day. A satin drape will cover the platform on which the coffin rests. Inside the platform, underneath the coffin, our little grandmother will be able to hide, safe as can be, whenever the need arises."

The bishop clapped his hands. Father Fernando smiled broadly.

"I like it!" the bishop exclaimed. "And what's more, I do believe it will work! But you need more than a coffin, my friend. You need a mannequin, clothing, lumber. Fernando, add to your list. We must get to work."

The Sunday edition of *El Diario*, the biggest news-paper in Saltillo, ran a front-page story about the plans of the three bishops to proceed with a request for early canonization for Maria Maristella Lopez, the young girl from Saltillo cruelly murdered in Texas by the drug cartels. The murderers were not named, as the editor feared for his life if he took that drastic step, but the story did state that the leading offenders were incarcerated in the United States.

Also given prominent coverage in the story was the bishop's plan to send the Miracle Bus to Louisiana on a pilgrimage in honor of the bus trip Maria Maristella took to save her young son. The bishop wanted the public to have a vested interested in the girl and her cause. The more attention the story got, the better.

The bishop also described his plans in his weekend homilies, offering his flock the opportunity to participate by donating toward the cause of the Miracle Bus. He was an eloquent speaker. His heartfelt words resonated with the congregation.

"Each and every one of us, no matter how poor or weak, has within us the capacity for selfless courage. Most of us, by the grace of God, never have to face such life-threatening situations. Maria Maristella, while still only a girl, saw what a truly evil man was doing to her young son. She knew the risk, yet her love was so great that she sacrificed herself to save her innocent child. This is the act of a true Christian martyr."

Maria Maristella had a nearly cultlike following of people who believed the bishop's words that she was a true saint and a martyr. They opened their hearts and their wallets and contributed to the cause.

The following Monday, Father Fernando, in his inconspicuous beige Kia, made his way to the home of Juan Diego. Riding along with him was the bishop's gardener who would drive Father Fernando's car back to the cathedral. Father Fernando was to drive Juan Diego's Miracle Bus to Saltillo to the garage of the mechanic Sancho Ramirez. Ramirez and his crew planned to give the engine a thorough going-over and make whatever repairs and adjustments were necessary. Father Fernando was astounded when he saw the gaily decorated bus. If the bishop wanted the bus to draw attention, his wishes were being carried out.

At the rectory on Monday morning, the money-counting ladies tallied up the special collection money. There was more than enough for a set of fine new tires and for several tanks of gasoline. The bishop also intended to buy Juan Diego two new pairs of khaki pants, two white shirts, and a decent pair of shoes. He had taken note of the homemade sandals the man wore and the callouses on his feet.

He made notes on these planned purchases then added, "Food for the journey. The fewer stops, the better."

The bishop called a parishioner who owned a clothing store. Within a few hours, a delivery truck arrived bearing clothing for Juan Diego plus a small mannequin with long, dark hair wearing a white confirmation dress and veil.

As directed, before Father Fernando left the garage, he removed from the bus all the paperwork he could find. The vehicle was still in the name of the previous owner, but there were receipts proving that the dead pastor had paid the man in full for the old bus. The bishop decided to go in person to deal with the official who could straighten out the problem and resolve the issue. He looked quite commanding when he put on his formal visiting attire.

The official dealt with the discrepancies in the title to the bus in short order. The bishop left the motor vehicle registration office with papers stating that the bus was registered to the Diocese of Saltillo. He and Juan Diego had decided that was the most expedient plan. The bus could be insured under the name of the diocese, and no questions would be asked, especially at the border crossing.

Juan Diego and Father Fernando planned to share driving duties, but Father Fernando would drive the bus across the border and answer all the questions. Dressed in his black suit with its white collar, he could present the

manifest listing all the passengers and he could show their tourist visas. With the grandmother safely tucked into her hiding place, the border patrol agents could enter the bus, check visas against identification, do whatever they needed to do. The bishop, who was greasing the wheels and preparing the way, didn't expect any problems.

Meanwhile, Juan Diego was studying diligently for his driving test. He must have a driver's license. It was his hope that the bishop might facilitate that as easily as he obtained the registration papers for the bus.

BAKERVILLE

The story about the canonization effort and the pilgrimage of the Miracle Bus also headlined the Sunday paper in Lafayette, Louisiana, the *Advertiser*. With a tip from the bishop, the editor had picked up the story from a wire service and deemed it worthy of publication, given the interest in the case in South Louisiana. Julia sat reading the story with wide eyes. When she reached the part about the Miracle Bus, she felt a bit faint. She decided not to mention it to Jon Teel to avoid having his hopes raised for no reason. At least once a week, he repeated his dream that his great-grandmother was coming on a school bus. Surely, the school bus that was making the pilgrimage was nothing but a coincidence. Still, she wondered.

SALTILLO

Juan Diego showed up for his regular visit with the bishop on a Monday morning. He had forgone his foraging trips as he worked on the bus. Today, he left Bonita and her cart at home because it was time to take his driving examination. He walked toward the back door of the bishop's residence preparing to knock when he noticed a terrible desecration. A large, copied photo of Maria Maristella, obviously made from the Sunday newspaper article, had been fixed to the door with a dagger dripping with blood. A large red X covered her face. Written in crude printing was a message:

> The traitor will never be a saint. Santa Muerte has spoken. Death to those who support her.

Juan Diego knocked frantically, bringing Father Fernando down the stairs in a rush. He too was horrified and called the bishop. The bishop, not overly agitated about the incident, called the police. They would be of no use, but at least he would put on a show for the perpetrators.

Before he allowed the mess to be taken away as evidence, he called the editor at *El Diario*. They sent a reporter and a photographer. This would be another front-page story with more attention drawn to the cause for sainthood and the pilgrimage of the Miracle Bus. All in all, the bishop was more pleased than upset about the unpleasant incident. He believed it to be the work of young hotheads in the cartel. He further believed that they were only shooting themselves in the foot. Actions such as this turned the people against them more than a Sunday homily ever could.

Once the matter of the bloody message on the door had been dealt with, Father Fernando took Juan Diego to apply for his first driver's license. The written test was difficult and took a great deal of time, but he was well-prepared. He had been tutored by Father Fernando who also taught him to drive the little Kia with ease. He went home that day with a new driver's license in his pocket.

The next morning, Father Fernando returned the bus to Juan Diego's place and handed him the keys. The engine was in top-notch condition, and the bus had brand-new tires—the best of the old tires they had reserved for spares. The men at the Ramirez mechanic shop had removed three rows of seats at the back of the bus. In the large empty space, they had placed the small coffin holding the white-clad mannequin.

Juan Diego was amazed when he opened the casket and looked at the mannequin. Someone had taken trouble with her wig, matching it to the newspaper photo of Maria Maristella. Her dress was exquisite, obviously quite expensive, made of fine white satin and lace. Her white veil was equally delicate and beautiful. Juan Diego was enchanted. The only problem, in his estimation, was her face. It was the waxy mask of a dress shop dummy.

Juan Diego got out his paint box, replenished with supplies from the bishop, and set to work. He protected her clothing with plastic bags. He painted her eyes closed then added long dark lashes. Looking at a copy of the newspaper picture of Maria Maristella, he shaped the lips with paint in a delicate shade of pink and colored and shaded the cheekbones to make an amazingly accurate replica of the girl's face. He stood back, critiqued his work, and had the good sense to stop before he ruined it. Now, he was ready to begin his carpentry work.

Using his old hand tools, he fashioned a simple wooden platform that fit across the back of the bus. He was a skilled carpenter, able to make exact calculations and cuts with crude tools. When he finished, the platform was a thing of beauty. Only a very skilled eye would detect that the front panel of the platform was removable. With the coffin containing the effigy of Maria Maristella sitting on top as a distraction, Juan Diego and the bishop both believed no one would even look.

He made a little shelf across the back of the bus, high above the wooden platform. On that shelf, he arranged some of his collection of religious artifacts. The Virgin of

Guadalupe statue was the centerpiece together with some of his Day of the Dead creations. These might scare off the bad people if, heaven forbid, they dared to enter the bus.

The bishop had sent along inside the coffin an old lace and satin altar cloth with which to drape the platform. He put the satin cloth in place. It covered the wooden platform nicely. Then using big wooden blocks to lift it in stages, he managed to maneuver the heavy coffin into place on top of the draped platform. He adjusted the satin drape, looked it over, opened the coffin to admire the mannequin one more time and decided it was as good as he could make it. In Juan Diego's personal estimation, he had created a perfect hiding place.

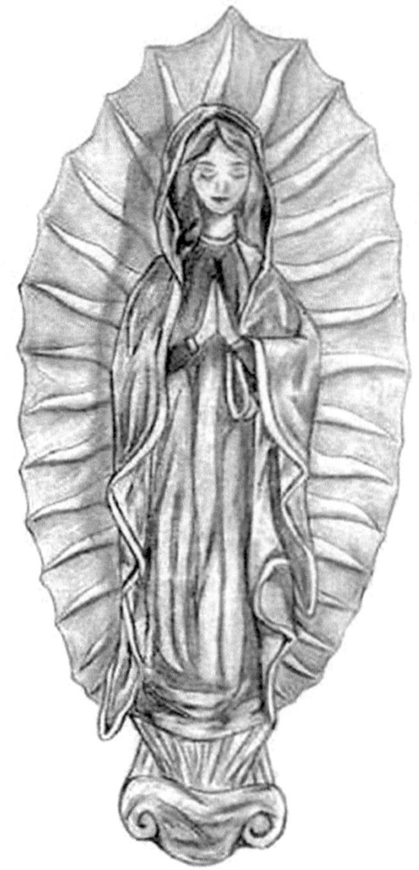

*****

In the days following the incident of the bloody message affixed to the bishop's door, the conspiring trio, including the bishop, Juan Diego, and Father Fernando, decided they were not overly concerned about the threat from the drug cartel. They had received no further messages. The blood, upon analysis, was revealed to be the blood of a goat. Still, they vowed to keep their guard up. They must be vigilant, especially when they began their journey on the bus. There were many uninhabited sections of highway. The bishop, using the bloody message affixed to his door as an excuse, requested a police escort for the bus as it traveled from Saltillo to the border crossing at Laredo. The authorities agreed. Local police and the federales would share the duty. This gave the trio a degree of peace of mind.

With the platform complete and the coffin in place, Juan Diego decided to leave the bus and take Bonita to town to do a bit of foraging and visit the bishop to set the date for the departure of the Miracle Bus. He had neglected Bonita and wanted to give her a little exercise and conversation. As they walked along, he shared his hopes and dreams for the pilgrimage with the docile donkey.

"Bonita, if you are a praying burro, please offer up prayers for us. We need them, my old girl. We are going on a big crazy adventure. If we succeed, it will be a beautiful thing uniting the old grandmother with her young great-grandson. We will be saving her life and giving her the grand opportunity of living her last days in peace with her only relative. But we need the bad guys to let us make our journey in peace."

Bonita gave a little snort as though in reply. They arrived at the bishop's residence. As Juan Diego reached up to knock, he shuddered as he noticed the scar from the dagger and the dark stain left by the goat's blood. He felt as though the cartel was not finished with them.

Father Fernando answered his knock and showed him up to the bishop's study. The three of them agreed that they would depart in one week on a Friday before first light. The drive to Nuevo Laredo would take four hours. They wanted to arrive at the border crossing by eight in the morning. If all went well, they would be many miles into Texas by noon. They would drive the bus straight to Bakerville to deliver Abuelita. They would spend two nights there. Parishioners in Bakerville were happy to provide housing for the visiting pilgrims. Julia Hancock had invited Father Fernando and Juan Diego to stay with her at Dapplefield Manor.

On their return trip, the pilgrims would make a stop in Houston to visit the archbishop who was planning a special Mass for them at the scene of the death of Maria Maristella. The abandoned boatshed was still encircled with crime scene tape, but the archbishop planned to erect a small altar outside the building and celebrate Mass with the group of pilgrims from Maria Maristella's home city.

Father Fernando had all their paperwork organized in a folder. He had the registration papers for the bus and the identification papers and tourist visas for each of the twenty passengers. Juan Diego had his new driver's license and a small new suitcase with one set of his new clothes packed. The other set of clothes he planned to wear. Juan Diego returned to his little home, happily anticipating the journey. Two of the people from the encampment planned to stay to guard their meager possessions. They readily agreed to watch Juan Diego's home and take care of Bonita.

At Sunday Mass, the bishop announced that the pilgrims would soon depart. He didn't give the date or time, not wanting to give the cartel that information. He simply told the congregation that the bus carrying members of the congregation would soon begin the pilgrimage to Texas and Louisiana to promote the cause of sainthood for their beloved Maria Maristella Lopez.

Something unprecedented happened in the cathedral after he made the announcement. The congregation rose and gave a long ovation. They began to chant, "Sainthood for Maria Maristella! Sainthood for Maria Maristella!" until the bishop motioned for them to be seated. He was overwhelmed by the fervent support.

THE JOURNEY

To avoid trouble at the time of the departure, the bus was left at Juan Diego's place in the country. Seven of the travelers plus Abuelita were living there already. The remaining pilgrims would depart from the cathedral at three-thirty in the morning on Friday for the drive to Juan Diego's place to board the bus.

Everything went according to plan. By four in the morning, they were on the highway. Abuelita was riding along like the other passengers but ready to get into her hiding place under the coffin at a moment's notice and certainly when they arrived at the border.

The police cruiser accompanying the bus traveled ahead, lights and siren fully engaged. The bus garnered little attention while it traveled through the dark hours, but at first light, travelers on the highway noticed the brightly decorated Miracle Bus with its police escort. They honked and waved. They also used their cell phones to notify their families and friends, and soon, there were people lining the highway as they passed through inhabited locales. Everyone

wanted to be a part of the cause for canonization of their own saint. Juan Diego's heart sang as he drove along. The bus was in top condition, the passengers happily singing all their favorite hymns and reciting the rosary.

One mile from the border crossing, the police vehicle inexplicably turned and made an illegal U-turn to return to Saltillo. The plan had been that the police would stay with them all the way to the border. This was worrisome, but they were nearly there.

Before they knew it, they were less than a quarter-mile from the border crossing at Nuevo Laredo. Some of the passengers assisted Abuelita into her snug hiding place. Father Fernando had taken the wheel some miles back. Juan Diego and Father Fernando exchanged glances, knowing they must remain calm.

At that moment, they noticed a large cloud of dust coming over the horizon from the west side of the highway. Soon, they could see that a black Humvee was approaching at a high rate of speed. The menacing vehicle swerved from side to side, jumped the protective curb on the side of the highway, and came to a stop, blocking the passage of the bus. They were now near enough to the border crossing that the guards could see plainly what was transpiring. They stood watching, not sure what to do. The passengers on the bus could see that a large crowd was assembled on the Laredo side of the border crossing, in the United States, awaiting the bus's arrival. They carried signs and banners, eager to support the cause of the little martyr.

Four young men in camouflage clothing got out of the Humvee, brandishing automatic weapons. A fifth man exited the vehicle, struggling to carry two five-gallon gasoline cans. They approached the door of the bus. Father Fernando, very frightened, refused to open it at their command.

"Let us in! The traitorous girl will never be a saint, and all who support her must die. What do you think, *compadres*? Should we shoot them and then burn them, or should we save our bullets and burn them alive?"

He aimed his weapon at the door of the bus, prepared to shoot it open, possibly killing Father Fernando in the process. Father Fernando reluctantly opened the bus door. Four of the assailants entered the bus, laughing at the frightened faces. It was apparent that they were nothing more than teenage bullies armed with powerful weapons. The leader walked down the aisle of the bus, brandishing his weapon, sometimes putting the barrel against the temple of a passenger. No one moved or spoke or challenged the intruders.

Then the terrified passengers began to pray softly together.

"Go ahead and pray, fools. Nothing but a miracle can save you."

The leader of the group walked to the back of the bus and looked at the coffin.

He took in the row of figures Juan Diego had placed on the shelf above the coffin.

"Day of the Dead? Yes, it will be the Day of the Dead for you fools."

He looked the coffin over.

"What's this?" he asked, "Is it ready for the first one of you that we kill?"

He opened the lid and jumped back when he saw the lifelike effigy of Maria Maristella. In the dim light, she appeared to be alive and only sleeping. Suddenly, from the coffin, a soft, disembodied voice spoke:

"Leave us in peace. Go now or die!"

Abuelita, in her hiding place, had decided she had not come this far to be murdered by a bunch of young thugs. The man backed down the aisle, visibly shaken.

"Let's go, guys, let's get out of here and set this big wreck on fire. No need to waste our ammunition on them."

The man standing outside the bus with the gasoline cans began to shout.

"Look! Trouble! Big trouble!"

They turned to see what would pass for a miracle that day. Traffic in both directions had been stopped by the standoff at the bus. Hundreds of people faithful to the cause for sainthood, who had been patiently waiting at the border crossing to greet the bus, broke through the gates and streamed toward the beleaguered vehicle. They filled the highway. To the five criminals, it looked as though an army were coming at them, all shouting and screaming.

The coward with the gasoline cans was the first to cut and run. He dropped the cans and ran for the Humvee. The leader looked at the rapidly approaching crowd of runners, fired a round of ammunition into the air, and followed his buddy, the others right behind him. They all climbed into their big, dusty vehicle and made a fast escape, a cloud of dust following them.

Police vehicles approached from the direction of Saltillo, better late than never. The police vehicle that had abandoned them would have some explaining to do. It was obvious that the officers had been bought off or threatened or both.

With much fanfare, the bus drove the remaining distance slowly, Father Fernando still trembling from his brush with death. Traffic on the highway remained stopped, allowing the bus to pass unimpeded. The huge crowd of supporters that had broken through the gates and run to

rescue the bus walked along beside the brightly colored vehicle, delighted that they were part of this historic event.

When they reached the border, Father Fernando presented all the legal papers. A border patrol agent made a cursory walk-through of the bus then allowed them to drive through to American soil.

A huge cheer went up from the crowd. The passengers were ecstatic. They believed they had been saved by a miracle. Abuelita remained in her hiding place, and for the moment, Father Fernando held on to the cellphones. They didn't need any glitches at this point.

The busy street they drove along after passing over the bridge and through the border crossing was lined with well-wishers, cheering them on. They drove slowly though the city of Laredo but quickly picked up speed once they left the city limits. Police units from each of the Texas towns and cities accompanied them, one picking up where another left off. Freer, George West, Beeville, Victoria, El Campo, all had police units waiting to take on the escort duty. When they neared Houston, a news helicopter hovered above, monitoring their progress. There was nothing like a story of poor good people triumphing over the bad guys to drum up viewership.

National television news channels picked up the story with the helicopter footage. The flower-bedecked bus with its shining adornments made for a great story. The helicopter flew near enough to get footage of smiling, waving passengers. The gold crosses shone at the front and the rear of the bus.

Soon, the big vehicle was exiting the sprawling urban area that was Houston, traveling on I-10 East. The passengers paused to pray as they neared the area of the boatshed—the killing place of Maria Maristella.

As they entered Louisiana, the bus pulled into the large rest stop provided by the state. Abuelita, who had come out of hiding as soon as the bus left Laredo, left the bus to stretch her legs and use the facilities with the rest of the passengers. She mingled in with them, as though she were one of the crowd. They were very close to the finish line. Father Fernando returned all their cellphones, only asking that they not reveal the presence of Abuelita just yet. After their ordeal with the young thugs, they readily agreed. They could keep the secret for a few more hours, with only 150 miles left to travel.

IN A TEXAS PRISON

News of the assault on the Miracle Bus reached the recreation room of a prison in Texas. Jonathan Steelman, never one to keep his mouth closed, cheered the assailants.

"Kill them all!" He screamed at the television. "Burn them alive!"

Prisoners of Mexican descent did not appreciate his sentiments. Except for Beast, aka Samuel Burleson, Steelman was a little man without followers in incarceration. His boasting and his general superior attitude won him no friends. Beast tried without success to separate himself from his unpopular former boss.

Later in the day, after the assault on the bus, Steelman was in a stairwell on his way back to his cell. He was in one of very few areas out of range of closed-circuit video cameras. A man unfamiliar to him came unnecessarily close. The man removed a thin plastic shiv from his sleeve. With lightning speed and surgical precision, he stabbed the shiv into the side of Steelman's neck, piercing his jugular vein. Jonathan Steelman had only moments to make his peace

before he bled out, alone on cold concrete steps in a Texas jail. If he ever repented, only God was aware of it.

Beast was judged guilty by association despite his attempts to separate himself from Steelman and to keep a low profile. He was harassed wherever he went in the prison. He lost weight because fellow inmates made meal-time a source of torture, none of it obvious to the prison guards.

It was common knowledge among the prison population that he was the one guilty of the torture and murder of Maria Maristella Lopez, sinking so low as to bite off part of her finger and, even worse, that of her son. These were the acts of a coward. Beast suffered inwardly, regretting the terrible acts he had committed in obedience to Jonathan Steelman's evil will. Beast began attending nondenominational religious services. He was truly sorry for his crimes, but he didn't expect God to forgive him. He believed in his heart that he was a lost soul. Still, he prayed every day for forgiveness.

At the same time as the attack on Jonathan Steelman, a second prisoner caught Beast alone in a hallway. This assailant had worked long and hard sharpening a length of oak pilfered from the prison wood-working shop. This perpetrator was not as kind or as skilled as the man who stabbed Steelman. As he passed Beast in the empty hall, he pushed the length of oak wood directly into Beast's shrunken stomach, then continued nonchalantly on his way.

Beast was found immediately after the attack and hauled off to the infirmary, bleeding profusely and praying out loud.

"Forgive me, Father God! I'm sorry! I'm sorry! Maria Maristella, forgive me! Help me, Maria Maristella!"

He repeated the words until he lost consciousness from blood loss.

Once the medical team got him on an examination table and cut his bloody prison uniform off, they were witness to a sight they could never erase from memory. They inserted an IV line to give him anesthetic and antibiotic drugs. They removed the wooden shiv then used sterile gauze pads to soak up blood from the jagged, gaping wound. As they cleaned the wound and prepared to stitch it closed, the pale edges of skin slowly began to close. A nurse had the presence of mind to get out her cell phone and start recording the miraculous healing of Samuel Burleson, the repentant murderer. The future St. Maria Maristella Lopez had performed her first recorded miracle.

BAKERVILLE

In Bakerville, preparations for the imminent arrival of the Miracle Bus were in full swing. The pastor had volunteers cooking and cleaning in the parish hall. There would be a welcoming supper, introductions, and the pilgrims would go to spend the night with their respective hosts. Parishioners had fought for the right to host a pilgrim. Everyone had seen the television coverage of the standoff before the border crossing—the brush with death for all the passengers.

Julia was at the parish hall helping when her cell phone alerted her that she had an incoming text message. It was from the sheriff saying only, "Call me. Urgent."

She walked outside the church hall to call Joe Blanchard.

"Julia," he began, sounding as though he couldn't catch his breath, "the Lord really does work in mysterious ways. The Mexican prison inmates in Texas didn't take kindly to the attack on the school bus. Jonathan Steelman couldn't keep his big mouth shut. He bragged all over the place that it was his men who did it. The other inmates never liked him anyhow. Bottom line, Steelman was stabbed to death today. Samuel Burleson was shivved in the stomach but managed to survive. Not only did he survive, but his wound healed shut on its own, and a member of the infirmary staff recorded the whole thing. He was calling on God and Maria Maristella to forgive him and help him, and I guess they came through. No one can believe it. But any threat from your boy's biological father is finally over. What a day! I'd like to give the guy who got rid of Steelman a medal."

Stunned, Julia could only reply, "Thank you for letting me know, Joe."

JOURNEY'S END

Led by police escorts all along the way, the Miracle Bus continued its triumphant passage through the towns in western Louisiana on I-10. All along the busy major highway, admirers of all races and religions lined up to wave and cheer the pilgrims on. Everyone wanted to be a part of the historic day. Once the bus reached Lafayette, where they traveled along city streets, the crowds grew. Abuelita felt safe now, sitting in a window seat waving at all the supporters. She sat on a pillow to have a better view. Juan Diego wondered at her tiny size. She had silver gray hair, olive skin wrinkled like an old walnut, piercing black eyes, and a smile that warmed the coldest of hearts. She had passed through the fire and survived.

The bus rolled into Bakerville by late afternoon. With the police escort leading the way, and traffic stopped for the occasion, the bus made a U-turn at the corner of Main and Adams Streets and rolled to a stop in front of Dapplefield Manor. All the parishioners from the parish hall had been alerted to the bus's arrival. They filled the front yard of

Julia's home, carrying signs and banners welcoming the pilgrims.

News of the apparent miraculous healing of Maria Maristella's murderer had spread through the group, adding to the importance of this day. The one bit of information that no one in Bakerville yet knew was the presence of Abuelita, great-grandmother of Maria Maristella, among the pilgrims on the Miracle Bus. The one person who was certain Abuelita would be there was Jon Teel, but he didn't voice his belief to anyone. He didn't want to jinx it.

Julia and Jon Teel waited front and center on the sidewalk as the bus came to a stop. Florida and her girls stood beside them. The double doors opened slowly, and Abuelita, despite her tiny size, descended the steps as regally as a monarch. She and Jon Teel locked eyes and ran to hold one another in a long embrace. A loud cheer went up as tears streamed down the faces of the observers.

"Abuelita! It's you! You're here! You came on the bus as you told me you would!" Jon Teel couldn't contain his joy.

BAKERVILLE

The joy of that reunion continued as the entourage of pilgrims descended from the bus to walk together to the church with the happy crowd. There, the pastor welcomed them and offered prayers of thanksgiving for their deliverance from their would-be attackers and for their successful journey. After, they walked over to the church hall where they enjoyed a typical South Louisiana dinner.

Everyone wanted to see the bus, the replica of Maria Maristella, and the hiding place that allowed Abuelita to scare off the villains and make her escape into the United States. They decided that the entire bus was a work of art. Juan Diego beamed silently and thanked St. Michael, the archangel. He also thanked Raphael, archangel or not.

*****

Several months passed as Abuelita found her place in Julia's household. She rapidly learned English. She became a minor celebrity on the streets of Bakerville as she frequently accompanied Julia or Florida when they walked Jon Teel to and from school. They continued to watch the progress of the mausoleum. Jimmie Daniel was particularly proud of his work as the bishop had added more requirements. The model of Maria Marisella was such a beautiful rendering that the bishop decided it must be displayed in a glass case sitting atop the crypt containing Maria Maristella's mortal remains. The bishop also wanted small windows installed, made of the same glass that protected the Pope in the pope-mobile. And it all had to be climate-controlled. All this took time. The funeral of Maria Maristella would not take place until all was in readiness.

Meanwhile, there was the matter of asylum for Abuelita. She had no papers of any kind with her. Although the bishop in Saltillo could not locate a birth certificate, he was able to find her baptismal certificate in the diocesan archives. He sent an official copy with the diocesan seal embossed and his signature. Judge Porteous Green facilitated the process. With Julia Chandler Hancock promising to sponsor Abuelita for the span of her remaining life, and given the definitive proof of the threat to her life in Mexico, Abuelita was given asylum and granted citizenship.

Everyone in Julia's household followed Jon Teel's lead and called her "Abuelita." When they went to Judge Green's chambers for the citizenship ceremony, they were amazed when Judge Green asked Abuelita for her given name and she replied, "I am the first but not the best. My given name is Maria Maristella. My last name is Sanchez. I am the grandmother of Maria Maristella Lopez, our little saint."

The grand funeral service for Maria Maristella Lopez finally took place once the mausoleum was completed. Scott Pellerin went to Baton Rouge early one morning to retrieve her skeletal remains. These he prepared for burial in the specially ordered casket which would go into the crypt in the mausoleum. Maria Maristella's mortal remains were ready for interment.

The archbishop of Houston planned to come for the day. The Bishop of Saltillo flew to the Lafayette airport. He planned to spend several days, so the rectory housekeeper readied a room for his arrival. The bishop of Lafayette also planned to help officiate. Three bishops concelebrating a service in the Bakerville church was unprecedented. So many of the faithful expressed interest in attending that the pastor arranged for big screen televisions to be installed in the church hall to accommodate the overflow. Scott Pellerin and the staff from Ibert's were the glue that held the service together. They knew how to make all the pieces of the elaborate ceremony come together as they should.

It was a moving funeral. Julia, Abuelita, Jon Teel, J-Max, plus Florida and her girls occupied the first pew.

The décor committee had outdone themselves with white flowers and candles massed on the main altar and the side altars. The bishop of Saltillo gave the keynote eulogy. His English was excellent, and his words eloquent. He described what he had learned of Maria Maristella from her former teachers, her sweetness, innocence, and pure goodness. The archbishop of Houston described the courage it must have taken for a young mother to defy a vicious gang and save her son. Finally, the bishop of the Diocese of Lafayette told of his gratitude that the last resting place of young Maria Maristella would be in his diocese. He spoke words of welcome, happy that Maria Maristella's grandmother and young son were making their home here.

"My friends," the bishop of Lafayette said, "let us use the example of young Maria in our own lives, always putting others ahead of ourselves, willing to risk all to save another."

The entire assembly walked outside to the mausoleum for the interment. Local law enforcement had to divert traffic away from Main Street; so great was the crowd who wanted to witness the moment when Maria Maristella was finally laid to rest.

After the day was over, Julia and her newfound family sat and recounted the events on the sunporch. This was Abuelita's favorite room. She had quickly adopted the habit of choosing a slip of paper from the Wise Sayings box. Sometimes, she waited for the group, but on several occasions, Julia had found her sitting near the box, struggling to translate the English words on a paper from the box. Today, Abuelita directed Jon Teel to choose a paper, which he eagerly did.

His small hand reached into the box, rummaged around, and finally selected a handwritten note: "Good wins out if we are patient enough to wait," he read.

"That's the best one yet," Julia said, beaming with pride at her family.

Once upon a time not very long ago, she had been a lonely widow. Now she had a big, loving family: Jon Teel, Abuelita, Florida, Orlie, and Waveland. She also counted J-Max and DJ. She looked around at the assembled group and gave a prayer of thanks.

ROME

Within the walls of the Vatican, behind a dark wooden door bearing the numbers 201, Pope Francis was enjoying his first cup of coffee in the hours before daylight and onset of the pressing duties of his day. He looked out the window of his apartment to the paving stones below. The first pigeons were arriving, looking for crumbs.

Like my flock, he mused, *always searching. We must assure that they are fed.*

He kept his finger on the pulse of the Roman Catholic Church all over the world. Three priests and two nuns had been kidnapped by rebels in Burkina Faso. Dreadful. An eighty-year-old nun in America had been jailed for gambling away nearly a million dollars that she embezzled from a Catholic school. Unbelievable. Surely, she had some mental defect.

The saga of the three bishops and the Miracle Bus drew his attention. He didn't approve of their flamboyant methods or their push for early canonization, but he did admire

their zeal. They were bringing fallen-away Catholics back
to the church.

However, the wheels of the church had turned very
slowly through the centuries. There was good reason for
such deliberate slow motion. It lessened the chance for mis-
takes. Nevertheless, he was anxious to meet in person with
the three bishops at the next general council meeting of all
the bishops in Rome. They had, after all, saved an innocent
old woman from a terrible death. That had to count for
something. The young woman who was murdered for saving
her young child seemed to meet the requirements for martyrdom. He directed his secretary to put the three men on
his calendar. He would reserve judgment until he was able to
meet them personally. He would, at least, hear them out and
give fair consideration to their request.